THE
DARK LAND

Jory Sherman

BERKLEY BOOKS, NEW YORK

This is a work of fiction. Names, characters, places, and incidents are either the product of the author's imagination or are used fictitiously, and any resemblance to actual persons, living or dead, business establishments, events, or locales is entirely coincidental.

THE DARK LAND

A Berkley Book / published by arrangement with
the author

PRINTING HISTORY
Berkley edition / July 2001

The Penguin Putnam Inc. World Wide Web site address is
www.penguinputnam.com

ISBN: 0-425-18066-2

BERKLEY®
Berkley Books are published by The Berkley Publishing Group,
a division of Penguin Putnam Inc.,
375 Hudson Street, New York, New York 10014.
BERKLEY and the "B" design
are trademarks belonging to Penguin Putnam Inc.

PRINTED IN THE UNITED STATES OF AMERICA

10 9 8 7 6 5 4 3 2 1

For Helen
A true pioneer woman and a wonderful writer

1

THERE WAS BLOOD ON THE LAND, THOUGH NONE COULD see it. None but Brad Chambers, who rode through it now like a man returning from the dead, like one who had crossed the River Styx and seen the skulls floating in its crimson depths, the shades of slaughtered men in its mists, the twisted expressions on the faces of men slain before their time, without any warning from God or the voiceless pickets lying where they had stood daydreaming before the sniper's rifle cracked the silence of a Texas dawn, before the lonesome cry of a curlew had floated over the solemn flow of soothing river waters.

He saw the dead and the dying, long after the guns had stopped cracking like whips; the empty-throated cannons stood like iron relics abandoned to the scavengers, and the white smoke had blown away like the ghostly shrouds of faded battleflags, turning to tatters and wisps before it vanished entirely over the corpses of faceless boys and men.

Corpses floated in the Rio Grande; the revelry had begun in Brownsville and across the border in Matamoros even before the last shot had been fired, even before the last man had fallen in a battle that should

never have been. Brad rode toward Brownsville with a
heavy heart, with an empty ache that could not be as-
suaged. The Confederacy was in shambles, his beloved
Cavalry of the West disbanded and the men scattered on
both sides of the border, some unwilling to surrender or
even to believe that the Confederacy had lost the war,
lost a month before that last fight when Lincoln had
accepted Lee's surrender at the Appomattox Courthouse
in Virginia, so far away Brad felt cheated that he was
not there to see it happen, to weep with General Lee's
men at the utter indignity of it all.

The dead Union soldiers had been strewn for seven
miles, shot down in their flight toward the Rio Grande
and not a Confederate soldier lost. He had seen the bodies floating in the Rio Grande—a sight so sickening, so
indelible, he could not erase the horrible images from
his mind. The faces of the dead floated in his memory
as they had floated on the big river and all of it so senseless, so unnecessary, so stupid.

And, now, Sheridan was in Brownsville, perhaps trying to sort it all out. The war was over, and the Confederacy had lost. But, there had been no formal
surrender on the Rio Grande. Men, even Colonel Rip
Ford, had just disbanded and drifted away. So, why had
General Phil Sheridan sent a courier with a message for
him to meet him in Brownsville? He was only a major.
Ford or Slaughter should have been the ones to be called
before the conqueror, but they were elsewhere, probably
over the border in Mexico as so many of his outfit were,
with dreams of joining up with Maximilian and fighting
the Mexicans.

Had Rip and the others not had their fill of war? Did
their blood run so hot it could not be cooled down, even
after a victory? They had defeated the Federals without
losing a single man. That should have been enough to
cause them to lay down their arms and accept the hon-
orable surrender that had been so generously offered
even before the last battle at Palmito Hill, even before

the fighting at Brazos Island, and now, once more by Phil Sheridan.

There it was again, unbidden, as always, since that last strange battle, and again, Brad turned his head quickly to see if he could catch a glimpse of it, that shadow that had been following him, that shade that had no name and no face and no form. And again, there was nothing there but the sallow sunlight and the faint aroma of burnt black powder still lingering in his nostrils, that sickly and elusive scent of blood and the sickeningly sweet smell of decaying flesh.

Was that shadow only his own conscience, left behind to stalk and taunt him like some remnant of battle smoke that no wind could bear away? Or was it the shade of some man he had killed himself, some searing stain on his soul that appeared and disappeared every time he thought of that last slaughtering charge when men tried to swim to the island and sank under the weight of their packs and rifles and pistols or were shot to pieces by stony-eyed Confederates crazed by the blood-lust that gripped men without warning in the heat of battle?

Shadows. They striped the road now, cast by the hui-sache grass and the stunted, windblown mesquite and live oaks, cast by his horse and his own figure, cast by the falling sun in retreat across the western sky, a bleak sun seeking the sea, deserting the plains. The sky would soon turn blood-red, leaving tattered banners of clouds turning to ash like burnt battle flags tacked to the distant horizon as reminders of what had happened here along the Rio Grande, of what had happened many times before ever since Brad had joined the Texas Rangers and met that bastard, John Salmon Ford in San Antonio, that exasperating, complicated, unpredictable man who had more courage in his little finger than most men had in their hearts and spines.

Old "Rest in Peace" Ford, his colonel, his father at times, his tormentor at others, a most baffling man whom he would have followed to his death, and damned

near did, but would now like to strangle with his bare
hands, because the man bore no allegiance to anything
or anyone, and might even turn up next as an enemy
whom he must battle, not on American soil, but across
the border, in Mexico.

Perhaps that shadow following him was Ford. Maybe
the colonel was dead, or maybe he was one of those
men who never died, but came back again and again to
fight every battle under a different name, in a different
body.

Brad rode through gathering shadows and looked over
his shoulder several more times as if knowing he was
being followed by someone, or something. But, he saw
only the blood-red horizon and the scarred clouds and
did not let his gaze linger on them because they might
contain faces or profiles of men he had killed or had
seen die, not just at Palmito Hill, but all across Texas
and into Mexico, long before the state had seceded from
the Union and he had left Sheridan to come back home
and defend Texas against men he knew and admired.

"Damn them all," Brad said aloud, as the lanterns and
torches of Brownsville came into view and the shadows
brought on a sense of dread of what Sheridan might want
with him, what he might say to a man who once served
with him and now was disgraced, another who had lost
a war that could not be won, a war that should never
have been fought.

But Rip Ford and the Cavalry of the West had won
the last battle. What would Phil have to say about that?
Would he gloat? He had beaten, somehow, an army that
had never been defeated. Texas had not lost its war. Its
war had been lost in the east, in Virginia, at Gettysburg,
and in Atlanta and Savannah and in Mississippi and all
along that bloody road that had begun at Fort Sumter.

Brad steeled himself for the meeting with General
Sheridan. Phil might look at him with scorn and want
to exact revenge, but he was not going to bow down to

Phil, nor show shame for his actions, nor cast aspersions on Rip Ford. He had fought for Texas, for his home, and he had not wavered in that fight.

He vowed he would not waver now.

2

BROWNSVILLE WAS TEEMING WITH PEOPLE: MEXICANS, civilians, Union soldiers, news reporters, boat captains and sailors, fishermen, women of the night, street vendors, children, and spies. Brad was challenged almost immediately by Union guards carrying rifles with bayonets fixed. The cantinas glistened in the glow of lantern light and the sounds of mingling people, twanging guitars, and raucous laughter spilled into the street. Some of the soldiers were drunk and staggered in and out of doorways as if they had lost all sense of place or direction.

"General Sheridan sent for me," Brad said, offering the piece of paper the courier had given him guaranteeing safe passage and entry into Brownsville.

Chambers had finely chiseled features that bore the tanned hue of sun and wind, a square jaw stubbled like his cheeks, long sideburns that were straight as froe-cut slabs of hickory, and a lazy smile that never quite left his curved lips. He stood near six feet tall in his socks and his wide shoulders emphasized his narrow waist and flat, hard stomach. He was lean and all muscle, and moved with a certain animal grace and quickness.

"You know where Union headquarters is?" the Corporal asked.

"Fort Brown, I suppose."

"General Sheridan's post is in town for the time being. You'll find him at the courthouse on the plaza."

"I know where that is," Brad said.

"Pass, then, you goddamned rebel."

"That's Major to you, Corporal."

"You ain't got no rank here," the corporal said.

"Thank you," Brad said, and rode by the guardhouse and down the main street until he came to the plaza at the center of town. He stopped in front of the building, the old courthouse flying the Union flag and Sheridan's colors, dismounted, and tied his horse to a hitch ring. Guards blocked his way, but after reading the note from Sheridan, let him pass inside. His boots made the boards creak. A single lantern glowed in front of a door at the end of the hall, where another Union soldier stood at relaxed attention. He stiffened when Brad approached.

"Major Chambers to see General Sheridan by appointment."

"May I see your papers, sir?"

Brad waited as the guard examined the note with the general's seal embossed on the paper.

"One moment, sir."

The guard knocked and a gruff voice told him to enter. The man stuck his head inside the door and whispered a few words. Then, he stepped back outside.

"You can go right on in, sir," the guard said. He did not salute and neither did Brad. Instead, the guard swung the door open and Brad filled it as he walked through.

A crusty sergeant sat at a desk in front of another door. He was surrounded by maps on the wall and his desk was stacked with vouchers, papers, an inkwell and quill pen, and wooden boxes holding still more papers. A battle flag stood in one corner and a rifle leaned against the wall behind the sergeant's desk. He did not get up.

"General Sheridan's expecting you, Chambers. He wants you to go right in." The sergeant flicked a thumb at the closed door. "Take off your hat when you get inside."

"Thank you, Sergeant."

The sergeant did not reply. Brad smelled whiskey fumes as he passed by the desk and lifted the latch on the door. Sheridan's office was filled with a pall of blue smoke and the strong aroma of cigars. But there was only one man inside—Phil Sheridan himself, who stood facing a map of Mexico and Texas on the wall behind him. He was framed by two flags like those outside, one Union, one his own regimental flag.

"General," Brad said.

"I told my men not to disarm you, Brad," Sheridan said, without turning around. "Were you treated well when you came into town?"

"Well enough, General."

Sheridan turned around. His keen look scoured Brad with a quick examination from boots to hat. Brad had not removed his hat when he had come in and Sheridan's gaze fixed on the CSA badge at the front of the battered crown. The hat was dirty and bloody, and had long since lost its original blocking.

It had been a long time since Brad had seen Sheridan and he did not notice much difference in his appearance, except he seemed more seasoned and those stars on his shirt made him seem taller, more powerful. If anything, Sheridan bore a distant resemblance to Colonel Ford, as if both men had been cut from the same sheet of iron. Certainly both men had a similar hard glint in their eyes, a fiery fervency that fairly shone in the boldness of their flinty glance.

"Major, eh, Brad?" Sheridan said, looking at the insignia on Chambers's shoulders. "If you'd stayed with me, you'd be at least a colonel by now."

Brad noticed two more doors in Sheridan's office, one on either side of the room. He could hear the gravelly

murmur of voices coming from behind the one on his
right. His gaze took in the bureau next to that door, with
its flask of brandy and a tray laden with glasses and
snifters. There was a porcelain pitcher, as well, white as
bone. Sheridan's sword hung from a peg on the wall,
and his hat dangled from a wooden tree in the corner.
Next to it, a Spencer carbine leaned against the wall, its
barrel and stock gleaming in buffed splendor from the
faint glow of the lamplight that sprayed from Sheridan's
desk.

"Begging your pardon, General, but my enlistment
was up when I left Missouri."

"Sit down, Brad, and let's not be so formal for a moment. It's good to see you after all these years. But
you're wrong about your enlistment in the Union army.
I took the liberty of keeping you on the rolls. In fact,
you have back pay coming. You can pick that up at the
quartermaster's."

"Sir, I don't understand."

Sheridan laughed, without any mirth. "I know a good
man when I see one. I knew the circumstances that
brought you under Colonel Ford's command. I knew that
someday that damned war would be over and I didn't
want the Texas Rangers to get you. So, you're still in
the Union army, Brad, and you've been promoted."

Brad stepped to a bare wooden chair and sat down.
Sheridan walked around to the front of the desk, placed
his buttocks on the edge, and leaned against the top as
he stretched out his legs, crossed the brown polished
boots, and folded his arms across his chest.

"You surprise me, General. I never figured you for a
man who would buck regulations."

"I was only a quartermaster when I got the call to
march with Henry Halleck on Corinth, over in Mississippi. You would have done well on that advance. I always liked the way you carried yourself, Brad."

"Yes sir, but I had a home in Texas."

"I know. I kept track of you."

"I kept track of you, too, sir."

"You used to call me Phil. You still can, you know."

"Yes, General."

"Brad, you're military, through and through, and now this war is over. I hope you do not bear me any ill feelings for my part in it. Nor for keeping you on the Union rolls."

"No, sir, I do not," Brad said. "But I am surprised. More than surprised, I guess. I may be the only man to serve in two opposing armies at the same time."

Sheridan chuckled. "You've been through a hell of a fight at Palmito Hill. You and that bastard Ford."

"Rip's a damned fine man, Phil."

"I know. But where is he? In Mexico?"

"I reckon so. Some of my friends don't want the war to end. They want to join up with the French and fight the Mexes."

"Yes. That's why I'm down here."

"Well, I plan to get on home, Phil. I've had enough of this madness they called the Civil War. Wasn't a damned thing civil about it."

"No." Sheridan unfolded his arms and paced a short distance in front of the desk. "Brad, I called you here because of two reasons. One, you are a man I can trust, and two, you were once a Texas Ranger, before you served with me in Missouri."

"I still am a Texas Ranger, Phil."

"I know, I know. But you're also a Union soldier. Well, the army has no use for Texas Rangers, as you know, but I'm the army here now and I have use for you. Don't buck me on this, Brad."

"I don't have much to offer," Brad said.

"I have an offer for you, however. I am appointing General Gordon Granger to command the occupying army of Texas. I am giving him fifteen hundred troops."

"Not many."

"I know. He's going to need some help. My intelligence tells me that some of the defeated Confederates are exacting retribution for the loss of their slaves, slaughtering Negroes and rich landowners. They are a tough bunch, mean as wild dogs, tough as hickory staves."

"I've heard that some are still fighting a lost war."

"I can't give you much help, and no official recognition beyond this office. But I'm appointing you colonel of an unofficial force of conscripts you choose to be under your command so that you can clear up this mess. I want you to hunt down every one of those butchers and either kill them, or bring them to justice before General Granger."

"You mean stand them up to a firing squad?"

"If that's what it takes to send a message to those renegades who won't give up until they've bathed themselves in innocent blood."

"That's a tall order, Phil."

"I know it is. Do you have any men you can attach to your outfit to help you carry out this thankless task?"

"I don't know. Two, three, maybe."

"Well, then that's all you'll have. I expect the Texas Rangers will be re-formed one day. Not right away, of course, but I'll do all I can to see that happen. And what you do for me will certainly play into the bargaining when I sit down with the Texas government."

"I'll do my best."

"You will draw a cash advance, separate from your back pay, from the paymaster at my post and henceforth, any funds you need will be provided by General Granger. Is that acceptable?"

"This advance. Is it army pay?"

"No, special pay for a special job. You'll still get army pay beyond that. It will be more than adequate. You can draw any arms and ammunition you need and you can also draw expense money from Gordon when you need it. Do you know him?"

"I've met him."

"I'll send you a letter of introduction, but show it only to him and no other."

"I understand, Phil."

"By the way, don't you want to know who heads up this bunch of scoundrels?"

"I do."

"Can you guess?"

"No, afraid not, Phil."

"He's an old friend of yours. An old adversary, really."

Brad's face drained of color.

"Not . . . ?"

"Abel Thorne."

Abel Thorne, Brad knew, had acquired a great deal of land by cheating Mexicans and Texans on a wholesale basis. He also knew that Abel's father had been a slave runner with Jim Bowie and his brothers before the war, then became a slaveholder himself. Brad knew the man well, for it was he whom Brad suspected of using Comanches to further his own interests, giving them whiskey and guns to wipe out families whose land he then got illegally.

"You know what happened to my family," Brad said.

"Yes. Comanches. Your wife and children. I'm sorry."

"I think Thorne was behind it."

"Then you have good reason to hunt him down, Brad."

Sheridan stuck out his hand. Brad took it.

"Bring Thorne in," Sheridan said.

"Alive?"

"Dead or alive. Clear?"

"Clear, sir."

Brad started to salute, then turned away. He knew Phil was not going to offer him a drink and he didn't want one anyway. He needed to get away by himself and think about what lay ahead. Thorne would not be easy to catch. He was as wild as any Comanche, and twice as ruthless.

Brad left the room and walked out of the building, onto the street. He stood there for a long moment, musing over his conversation with General Sheridan.

It was funny, he thought, how life had a way of chasing you in a circle. He had thought the war was over, but it was not. It had only taken a different turn. Maybe, he thought, this war would never end. To warriors like Sheridan and Ford, that was good news. But, to Brad, it meant that someday he might see a face on that shadow that kept following him.

3

Brad stood there, outside Sheridan's headquarters, listening to the sounds of Brownsville, wondering if he should put up for the night or ride out of town and spread his bedroll under the stars, away from people.

"Major Chambers?"

Brad turned at the sound of his name and saw a smartly dressed Union corporal standing next to him, holding a packet under his left arm.

"I'm Chambers."

"Begging your pardon, sir, but the general forgot to give you this packet. He apologizes for his forgetfulness. Here are your orders, a letter to General Granger, some cash, and a voucher for a night's billet in town, sir."

Brad took the packet. "I doubt if General Sheridan forgets anything, Corporal." The corporal saluted and turned on his heel without waiting for Brad to return the courtesy.

Brad walked over to stand under a lamp as he opened the packet. He read the orders quickly, pocketed the paper money, and turned to one of the sentries. At least he knew now why Phil hadn't given him the packet in his office. Phil was ordering him to report to Granger

immediately and come under his command. Sheridan
must have known that Brad didn't like Granger. He
wondered now if he could have turned Phil down and
decided, in light of the assignment, that this would have
been stupid of him. He badly wanted to find the man
responsible for the murder of his wife and daughter, and
this afforded him the opportunity to hunt down Thorne
legally and get paid for it. He was still owed back pay
from the Confederacy, pay that he knew he would never
receive.

"Where's the Rio Grande Hotel?" he asked.

"Down the street and around the corner," the sentry
replied. Brad folded the voucher, then walked to his
horse and untied it from the hitch ring. He walked to the
hotel and saw that there was a stable nearby. He put up
his horse and told the stable boy to grain and groom
him. That, too, had been paid for by the U.S. Army.

He checked into the hotel, threw his bedroll on the
bed, and read his orders again, more carefully this time.

"Granger," he said to himself. "At least I won't have
to see him but this one time."

In the morning, he was on his way to Galveston to
meet General Granger. He left before dawn to avoid
the heat, and he tasted the tangy Gulf breezes, watched
the seagulls wheel in the cloudless sky of morning after
the fog had lifted.

He thought of Sheridan's letter to General Granger
and got a bad taste in his mouth. He had met Granger,
once, and had not liked the man. Now, he would be
under his direct command. He wondered how Granger
would take to that idea. Brad sensed that the general
would not be a benign conqueror, that he would shoot
any man he suspected of wrongdoing without benefit of
a court-martial. But Brad would do anything to track
down Abel Thorne, if he was the man responsible for
sending the Comanches down on his family.

*Smoke in the air, its shadow on the ground like some
ominous stain. The smell of burning wood. The wind*

making whispers in the grasses like lost voices trying to make him hear. Clear blue sky, not a cloud in sight.

The knot in his gut kept tightening as he rode closer to the ruins of what had once been his home, and he rode into the shadow of the smoke and became part of it and the wind low along the ground, the smoke hanging there like some warning flag over the remains of the house, which stood like a scarred skeleton, roofless, only the chimney and the four pillars at its corners, like tall grave markers.

The black loam of the earth muffled his horse's hoofbeats, loam laced with sand, and the ground around the house scorched, the huisache grass singed and dying, the blades bent and twisted into grotesque shapes.

Mary had the yellowest hair, like straw spun from gold and drenched in sunshot honey, and his gut tightened even more as he rode toward the barn, still standing, as if it had been spared to act as a landmark to the tragedy that had occurred here. Little Lucy, too, with that same kind of soft hair, and he could see his daughter's eyes in that blue of the sky and around the fringes of the smoke shadow, the hazel tones of Mary's eyes, and he felt his throat constrict as if it had been rubbed with sand and lye.

He saw the furrows on the ground where they had dragged his wife and daughter. The tracks led to the barn and the big doors were gaping open like some obscene maw. Inside, he saw them both, their bodies torn and mutilated, almost beyond recognition. The plow horse and the two cows were gone. Lucy's corpse lay before an open stall and Mary's remains had been thrown over a sawhorse like a blanket. Both bodies were bristling with arrows as if they had been used for target practice by the young bucks.

The arrows bore the markings of the Comanche tribe. Each had a drawing of a turtle to show they were owned by that warrior clan. The smell of death was thick. The Comanches had cut away the private parts of the two

*women and Mary's breasts were carved from her chest,
sliced off neatly so that he knew she must have been
dead when they did that to her. Lucy's chest was
smashed in and her ribs broken and splayed back. Her
little heart was gone, cut out of the dark cavity as if
plundered by some insane demon, bent on robbing her
of her very soul.*

General Gordon Granger had arrived in Galveston on
June 19, 1865, and announced, in the name of President
Andrew Johnson, that Texas was now under the authority of the United States government and that all black
slaves were thereby freed from their white masters.

The Negroes proclaimed that day Emancipation Day
and celebrated it thereafter as "Juneteenth," in honor of
their freedom.

Granger further proclaimed that all acts and laws of
the Confederacy were now null and void and he would
brook no resistance from any quarter.

Brad Chambers waited outside Granger's office in
Galveston, annoyed that he had to report to a man he
thoroughly disliked. He did not then know that the feeling was mutual.

If he could have heard what Granger was saying to
his adjutant at that moment, Brad might have left without seeing the general, no matter what the consequences
might be.

"Farley, I don't know what Phil was thinking about
when he put together this mission."

Captain Ned Farley coughed, but said nothing.
Granger was reading the orders for the fifth or sixth time
that afternoon.

"I hate Texas Rangers and Brad Chambers even more.
Chambers is a disloyal lout who deserted the Union
Army to join that renegade Rip Ford. I wouldn't trust
the man to hunt bunny rabbits at Easter."

"Yes, sir. Major Chambers is still waiting outside."

"I know, Farley, I know. Let him cool his heels out
there. I met Chambers once and didn't like him on the

spot. He's not military by any stretch of the imagination. He's a damned cowboy, an arrogant Texian, and was probably a damned slaveholder before the war."

"I wouldn't know, sir."

"If I had my say, Chambers would be charged and brought before a court-martial. And Ford would be shot on sight."

"Yes, sir. I understand, sir."

"Farley, you don't understand a damned thing. You don't know how deep my feelings go regarding the war and those damned rebels. President Johnson wants these scoundrels treated with courtesy and respect. But he wasn't fighting in the war and he doesn't know what we went through. Chambers represents everything about the South that I abhor. He's disobedient, disloyal, and an opportunist."

"Sir," Farley said, leaving off the affirmative.

"Well, send Chambers in, and then I want you to tell Coy to come here after I've finished."

"Yes, sir, I'll attend to it."

Farley opened the door and beckoned to Brad, who got up and walked toward him, carrying the packet in his left hand. Farley looked at the pistol hanging from Brad's belt in a tooled leather holster, and then looked up at the man as he passed, startled at how tall Chambers was. "General Granger will see you now, Major."

Brad didn't reply, but entered the room.

"General Granger, I have a letter for you from General Sheridan."

"Let me have it, Chambers. Then you stand at attention while I look it over."

The general stood in front of his desk. He took the letter and scanned it quickly, then threw it behind him on the desk.

"You're not going to take up a lot of my time, Chambers, so I'll get to the point. You are authorized to draw money from the paymaster, and supplies from the quartermaster. You have your orders. You are to act on behalf of the U.S. Army and bring in any prisoners you succeed in taking. You are to send regular reports to me and you are to report only to me, is that understood?"

"Understood, sir."

"Frankly, I don't expect much of you. These renegades who are raiding farms and ranches in the Rio Grande Valley are smart and they move fast. The only reason General Sheridan picked you is because you know the country and you apparently are acquainted with the leader of this band of scoundrels, Abel Thorne. I believe he is a friend of yours."

"No, sir, Thorne is not a friend of mine."

"But you know him."

"I know him as a horse thief and a Comanchero."

"What in hell's a Comanchero?"

"Sir, he's a white who took up with the Comanches."

"Well, from what I've seen of this godforsaken state of Texas, we ought to give it back to the redskins."

Brad did not reply, but stood at attention. His nose itched, but he wasn't going to give Granger the satisfaction of seeing him scratch it.

"Well, you'd best get to your duties, Chambers. Let me give you fair warning, though."

"Sir?"

"If you fail in your obligation to this command, or if you decide to desert and join the renegades, I'll have you hunted down and shot on sight, without benefit of a court-martial. Understood?"

"Perfectly, sir."

"Very well, then. Dismissed."

Brad saluted smartly. He waited for Granger to return the courtesy, but the general turned his back on Brad and walked to the window, gazing out at the small parade ground behind his office. Some men were marching, while others were performing close order drills. Brad left the room and asked the corporal on guard to direct him to the paymaster's office.

"First things first," he said.

"Beg your pardon?" the corporal asked.

"Never mind. I'll find it."

Brad left and saw two men leave the shadows of a barracks awning and walk briskly toward headquarters. He made note of both their faces, but knew he had never seen either before. One was a corporal, the other a lieutenant. The lieutenant was the one who made eye contact with Brad and his gaze never wavered until they had passed several yards apart.

Brad made note of that brief exchange, too.

A few moments later, he stopped and scratched his head. That lieutenant, he thought. There was something familiar about him. But, try as he might, he could not place the man's face just then. Yet Brad knew he had seen him somewhere before, under different circumstances.

"It'll come to me," he said to himself, and continued walking toward the paymaster's office in one of the clapboard buildings that made up Granger's post.

Just before he walked inside, he stopped again, struck with a sudden thought and a nagging premonition.

"And I'll bet I see that shavetail again," he said, half aloud. "Damn Granger anyway."

4

GENERAL GRANGER LIT HIS PIPE AS THE DOOR OPENED.

Lieutenant Jared Coy entered alone.

"Did you see Chambers?" Granger asked.

"Yes, sir, I saw him."

"Did he recognize you?"

"No, sir, I do not think he did."

"Good. Then he doesn't know you fought against Ford and Slaughter at Palmito Hill."

"He wasn't one of those I chased across the Rio Grande, General."

"No, I don't believe Chambers was chased anywhere by anyone."

"Sir, the captain didn't tell me why you wanted to see me. Was it regarding Major Chambers?"

"Sit down, Jared. Do you smoke?"

"No, sir, not regular."

Coy sat in one of the chairs. Granger took another and moved it close to the lieutenant.

"Nothing like a good pipe to calm a man down when his blood's running hot." Granger leaned forward in his chair. "Jared, I consider Major Chambers nothing more than an outlaw, a bounty hunter serving temporary duty in the United States Army. What are your feelings about him?"

"Sir, I know he can ride a horse right well."

"Well, Phil Sheridan thinks Chambers is the man to stop those depredations by a man named Abel Thorne. I'm not so sure. I have an assignment for you, but first I want to know if you have any feelings about Chambers. I want to know if you still consider him your enemy, or if you think he has learned his lesson."

"Sir," Coy said, "I know Chambers to be a rebel and if we were at war, he would be my enemy."

"The Civil War may be over, Jared, but the fighting's not done. Those rebels you chased into Mexico want to continue it by making either the French or the Mexicans into allies. I think Chambers bears no loyalty to the Union. I consider him a threat to the peace. How about you?"

"Sir, if I could have chased him across the Rio, I would have. And if I had gotten him in my sights, I would have shot him dead."

"Well, that's good enough. I don't trust Chambers. I want you to track him. I want you to go where he goes, is that clear?"

"Yes, sir. But . . ."

"If Chambers steps out of line just once, you are to put a bullet in him. Understood?"

"Consider it done," Coy said, unable to mask his delight at the assignment.

"Take along a squad of your best men, supply yourself for a month in the field."

"Yes, sir. I know just the men to take with me."

"I know you will do your duty, Jared. These are verbal orders only, so you must be discreet. I don't want Phil Sheridan down on my back."

"I understand, General."

"You'd best get going, then. I have no idea where Chambers will go first, but my guess is he will probably go back to his ranch and recruit some of his rebel friends to help him go after Thorne."

"Yes, sir, I expect that's what he'll do. I have a good tracker who can follow a snail's tracks on wet grass."

Granger smiled.

"You'll do, Jared. I'm counting on you to be my eyes and ears, and, perhaps, Chambers's judge and jury."

Coy rose from his chair and nodded to the general.

After Jared Coy left the room, Granger sat in his chair for several moments, puffing on his pipe.

He hoped Chambers would slip up. And if Coy did what he was expected to do, he'd be wearing captain's bars shortly after his return to the post.

5

TWELVE DAYS AFTER HE LEFT GALVESTON, BRAD CHAM-
bers crossed the Nueces River, then headed for what was
left of his home, not far from Kingsville. He rode a route
that would take him to the various ranches he knew, so
that he could begin looking for the friends he wanted to
ride with him as he hunted down Abel Thorne.

The memories of that last battle were still vivid and
strong in his mind and, as he rode, he saw the destruc-
tion left behind by the Union Army as they rode south
toward the Rio Grande. He had no idea that they had
taken a cue from Sherman's march through Georgia, but
there was scorched earth to prove it. The longer he rode,
and the more he saw, the angrier he became.

But he also became more reflective as he realized that
Colonel Ford had actually been responsible for the first
shots fired in the Civil War, even though few knew
about it. Brad remembered well how he had come to be
involved in that first engagement not far from where he
now rode.

He could still see Ford's crackling blue eyes and hear
his blistering, imaginative blasphemy, even though he
had not cursed when he came to recruit Brad for his

damned Cavalry of the West. Rip could speak with all
the honey-tongued skills of a diplomat when he wanted
to, and inspire a man's heart to beat faster with his simple, straight talk that needed no colorful swear words to
infect a man with his persuasive powers.

*There was not much to the man. He was almost fifty,
then, and Brad had thought he must already be dead.
He had already lived more lives than most men, as a
medical doctor, lawyer, newspaper reporter, a senator
who had served two terms in the Texas legislature,
mayor of Austin, and a captain in the Texas Rangers.*

*"I want you to join an outfit I'm putting together,
Brad,"* John Salmon Ford had said that day as he rode
up to what was left of Brad's ranch.

"I'm already in the U.S. Army."

"You are also a Texas Ranger."

"Not anymore. Neither are you."

"I'll always be a Ranger, Brad. So will you."

"What kind of outfit are you putting together?"

"A regiment of cavalry," Ford had said. *"We're going to fight the Union on the Rio Grande. And I'm sorry
about what happened to your family."*

"Look, Captain, I don't hold to this war much."

*"You've already got blood on your hands, Brad. Phil
Sheridan speaks very highly of you."*

"You know Phil?"

*"I know him some. When he was quartermaster, I sold
him a few goods."*

"He's a Yankee. Why would he tell you where I was?"

*"He doesn't know I'm a Confederate colonel now. He
knows you and I were Rangers."*

"A colonel?"

*"That's what they made me, Brad. I could use you,
Major."*

"Major?"

*"That's the rank you'll hold in the Cavalry of the
West."*

Ford looked around at the ruined house, the pecan

trees, the persimmon grove, the live oaks and the remnants of mesquite that still held to the soil that now grew grass to a man's knee.

"You know, Rip, I was wonderin', before this happened, if I'd ever be called upon to fight against Texians."

"Phil told me you were restless. He figured, after you heard what happened to your family, you wouldn't be back."

"He did?"

"He said that to someone who told me."

"A spy, you mean."

Ford smiled wryly. "A friend in the Union Army."

"I don't think you talked to Phil Sheridan at all. He's a pretty smart man. He'd know you were a Confederate."

"Well, let's say I knew you'd be here and I came to make an offer. I can use you. Texas needs you. And the fighting's going to be right near here, unless I miss my guess."

"A blockade isn't fighting."

"No, but when those cotton wagons come down to the river, the Federals are going to want to keep them from loading. Oh, we'll be fighting, all right. Federal troops on Texas land."

"Sheridan expects me back," Brad said.

"No, son, he doesn't."

"Damn you, Rip."

Rip Ford smiled again and Brad got the feeling that the slightly built jack-of-all-trades knew more than he would ever tell, about everything worth knowing.

"I've just buried my wife and daughter."

"I know. And you'll bury more good folks if you don't come with me and join my cavalry."

"The South is going to lose this war, Rip."

"Brad, I'm not going to lose. I'm not going to lose even one son-of-a-bitching battle."

And he had gone with Colonel John Salmon Ford,

knowing he would never be able to explain why.

He was relieved to see the house in the distance, still standing, surrounded by live oak and clumps of mesquite kept there to block the wind and soak up the dust before it ransacked the house with grit when the winds blew fierce from the Gulf and from the west, that long hot western wind that moved land around so that it was always changing, and what dirt didn't land somewhere, clogged a man's throat and eyes and nose and ears until he was blind, deaf, and dumb.

As he drew closer, he was surprised to see Gid's house still standing. But he sensed something was missing, even so. After his own tragedy, he expected that no other's home would remain intact. It was dumb of him, he thought, but the shock of seeing his own place burned to the ground had left him cockeyed.

"Hello the house," he called when he passed the mesquites. He reined up and waited to be recognized before he rode any further.

"Gid?" he yelled.

He surveyed the house, looking for signs of life. He stared beyond it, and his stomach tightened. His jaw hardened and a muscle quivered from the tension of his clenched teeth. Once, there had been a long field of cotton growing behind Gideon Tunstal's home. Now, it was scorched black and only a twig or two jutted up from the ground.

He shifted his gaze to another area where a stand of live oaks stood surrounding a green island of grass. His blood froze when he saw the white cross. That was the place Gid had picked to be the family graveyard. He had lovingly planted the grass and his wife, Emily, had tended it over the years, putting in bordering flower beds. The flowers were still blooming, Brad saw, bluebonnets and yellow daffodils and clusters of peonies.

Brad ticked the mare's flanks with his spurs and she stepped out. He guided her to the lone grave and halted when he was close enough to read the words on the cross. There was no name. But someone had written a line in small block letters, painted them with a brush, actually.

"I loved her," was all that it said.

"Brad?"

Brad turned and saw Gideon walking toward him, a scattergun in his hands. His clothes were filthy, a pair of rumpled duck trousers held together by wrinkled galluses, a shirt stained with food and sweat, once a light blue, but now dark with grime and unknown substances. Gid was barefoot and hatless, his face flocked with a matted beard and mustache, and his hair long and untrimmed. If it were not for his pale blue eyes, Brad might not have recognized him.

"Gid, what the hell happened here? That's not Emily buried there, is it?"

"They come in the night, Brad, the sons-of-bitches, whilst I was out at the pump. One of 'em coldcocked me with a billy made of ironwood. When I come to, Emily was beat half to death and my cotton burnt to a crisp."

"Jesus, Gid."

"Light down, Brad, for God's sake, and let me put hands on you. Ain't nothin' been real for me in a long time."

Brad swung out of the saddle.

"Lemme put your horse up, Brad," Gid said, reaching for the reins. "Damned if you ain't a sight for sore eyes."

"I'm sorry about your wife, Gid."

"I done cried her all out of me, but I miss her somethin' terrible."

The stock tank back of the pond was stagnant, limned with a thick green scum dotted with black ash from the burnt cotton fields. Gid put Brad's horse in a stall, stripped it of saddle and bridle, and handed Brad his bedroll and saddlebags.

"I've got money to buy horses, food, and gear," Brad

said. "I was just waiting to see if you'd ride with me first."

"What for?"

Brad told him all that had happened at Fort Brown and in Galveston.

"Maybe it was Abel Thorne what burned my cotton up."

"Or somebody just like him."

The two walked to the house and went inside. The rooms were all in disarray and the kitchen a mess. Gid made coffee and Brad threw his bedroll and saddlebags on a bunk in a spare room, which was more tidy than any other. He and Gid sat at the table between the front room and the kitchen and listened to the pot boil. Gid cut off a chunk of tobacco from a twist and popped it into his mouth. He offered the twist to Brad, who shook his head.

"Wish old Rip was here," Gid said. "He would tear Thorne a new asshole."

"Ford disappeared," Brad said. "I think he went south."

"Ha, he might do that, the old blue-eyed buzzard. 'Member when we chased Ochoa out of the country back in sixty-one? That bastard didn't know what he bought into when he hanged that county judge in Zapata and declared war against the Confederacy."

Brad remembered it well. Ford's cavalry killed twenty of Ochoa's men and some said that was the first battle of the Civil War, down along the Rio Grande.

"Well, we got some chasin' to do ourselves, Gid," Brad said.

"You and me?"

"I've got in mind two more of our friends."

"Who?"

"Randy Dunn and Lou Reeves."

Gid whistled. Then he got up from the table and pushed the pot away from the fire and closed the damper. He poured two cups of steaming night-black coffee and brought them to the table. "Ain't got no sorghum nor sugar, Brad."

"Black's fine."

"I heard what the Comanches done to you and your missus and kid. I'm awful damned sorry."

"Thorne's a Comanchero, you know."

"I heard tell."

"He may have sicced those dogs on my place."

Gid drank from his cup and slapped his leg with glee. He grinned wide. "Brad," he said, "you see that scatter-gun I leaned up against the wall?"

"The one you threw down on me with a while ago?"

"Same one."

Brad looked at it again. It was an old Greener, a double-barreled caplock. He saw where Gid had tried to scrape away the rust. The barrels were two different shades of brown, at least.

"What about it?"

"Just before you rode up, I had it in my mind to put both barrels under my chin and blow my brains out."

Brad looked at Gid, who was no longer smiling.

"That bad, huh?"

"Captain, I think you done saved my life."

"Gid, you may not be so grateful once we get on Thorne's track. He's a mean one."

"Well, you know, I thought about such all through the war. Killin' and all. And I come to a conclusion."

"Yeah, Gid? What was that?"

"I figger sometimes killin' is what keeps a man alive."

"That's a hell of a conclusion, Gid."

"I know, I know. But that old Greener didn't get me. I'll ride with you, and Dunn and Reeves, Brad, and if I get killed, you bring me back here and bury me right next to Emily."

Brad nodded, but didn't say anything. He was glad he had decided not to tell Gid or the others that he was a Union soldier, drawing army pay. That would be difficult to explain. He was glad, too, that he had not been ordered to wear a Union uniform. But being deceptive to his friends was not in his nature, and he felt uncomfortable keeping such a big secret. The coffee was hot and he blew on it before he took a sip. He looked out the window at the scorched fields, then back to the scattergun leaning against the wall by the door.

A man could only take so much, he thought.

6

BRAD WATCHED GIDEON TAKE THE STRAIGHT RAZOR to his beard and begin carving away at it. Gid's beard was snowy white with lather, and he dipped the razor into a bowl of water and shook it to clean it each time he sliced off a new tuft.

"When I pick up Lou and Randy, I'll take you all to a place where I cached some new rifles and cartridges I got from the army," Brad said. "But bring your own rifle. There's new scabbards in the cache, too."

"What kind of rifles?" Gid asked, as he slashed a large chunk of hair off his face.

"Spencer repeaters. Carbines. Brass cartridges."

"Always wanted one of them. I saw you had one in your saddle scabbard. Mighty fine little rifle."

"How'd you like to pack a Colt, too?"

"I'd like that a lot, Brad. That one on your belt?"

"Yep, a .44."

"I noticed the bullets, figured them to be .44's. All shiny and brand new."

Brad reached down and opened one of his saddlebags. He lifted out something wrapped in oilcloth and set it on the table. Then he reached back in and dug out a box of .44 cartridges and set them next to the bundle.

"We might have to live off the land on this expedition."

"Hell, I'm doin' that now."

"I figure Randy and Lou might be living around here."

"Yeah, Randy's got him a spread up yonder and Lou ain't no more'n ten or twelve miles from him."

"I hope they'll ride with us," Brad said, remembering back to that day when Rip Ford gave him the assignment to go after Ochoa.

When the scouts, Sergeant Louis Reeves and Sergeant Randolph Dunn, had made their report, Colonel Ford was ready to draw some blood.

"Corporal Stevens," he called, "fetch Captain Chambers in here and light a fire under your soft ass."

Reeves and Dunn suppressed smiles.

"So, you found Ochoa here in the Zapata region between here and Laredo, eh, Lou?"

"Yes, sir. Right where I showed you on the map."

"That goddamned greaser's fucking up my command here. We need this gateway to Matamoros and I'm not going to let some two-bit bandit muck it up. Randy, how many men does Ochoa have under arms?"

"Near as I can figger, sir, he's got maybe thirty-five or forty fighting men, a few Mex whores, and some boys with machetes. Maybe fifty head all told."

Ford turned to see Brad Chambers stride through the open door, his new captain's bars glinting as he stepped into the light streaming through the window in Ford's office.

"Brad, you know these scouts," the colonel said.

"I wouldn't claim it outside present company, Rip."

"You fuckin' Texians," Ford said. "I'll bet you're all goddamned cousins."

"I don't claim relations to these two," Brad said. "But I'd ride the river with either or both."

"They found that little Mex bastard Ochoa down here, along the Rio Grande. He's a thorn in my side and I

want you to take a troop over toward Zapata way and
tear his bunch a new set of assholes. You take Dunn and
Reeves along to show you where he is."

"The men are ready to ride," Brad said.

"Well, I want 'em ready to shoot, too."

"They are that, Colonel."

"Lou, are you and Randy rested up enough to ride
out with Captain Chambers?"

"Sir, we slept in our saddles on the way back."

"Get your asses out of here, all of you. Brad, I want
Ochoa driven so far into Mexico he can't find his way
back, hear?"

"I understand, sir."

"You know, Brad, this could very well be the first
battle of this damned Civil War, don't you?"

"Well, you already won the first battle when you ran
Fitz John Porter out of Fort Brown."

"But I did it with words, not powder and ball."

"It was a victory, nevertheless," Brad said.

Ford grumphed and his blue eyes crackled with lam-
bent sparks.

"Porter had one ball the size of a pissant, Brad. The
other one was an itty-bitsy one."

Brad laughed.

"My troop is just waiting for 'Boots and Saddles,'
Rip. You through with me?"

"Do me proud, Brad. I'd go with you, but I've got a
cadre of alcaldes and minor officials ragging my ass."

"You'll make a fine administrator, Rip."

"One of these days, I'll give you a lesson in sarcasm,
Brad. Yours don't have much sting."

Ford waved Brad out of his office.

Brad waded through the pack of Brownsville digni-
taries waiting for an audience with Ford in the outer
office. They were all dressed in tight-fitting suits and
stiff-collared shirts, with boots that shined like mirrors.

"Where you going?" one of them asked.

"None of your business, sir," Brad said and the whis-

*pers rose up in his wake as he left headquarters and
stalked after his bugler to order him to sound "Boots
and Saddles."*

"We can do some scouting along the way. I want to
try and pick up Thorne's track right quick."

"If he's with the Comanches . . ."

"I thought about that. I ran into a man on the way
here who heard tell of Thorne. He said he was riding
with a bunch of white men. Thieves, he called them."

"From what I know of Thorne, all of his friends are
thieves. He didn't fight in the war, you know. He raided
farms and ranches the whole time."

"I know."

Gid finished paring down his beard. He stropped his
razor, lathered his face again with soap, and started peel-
ing off hair down to the skin.

"Just about done," Gid said. He was working without
a mirror, by feel only, and Brad thought he was doing
a pretty good job. The face he knew from the cavalry
was slowly emerging from under the beard.

Brad took a piece of paper and a stub of a pencil out
of his pocket. He began to write on the paper, drawing
lines and circles and X's. Then he wrote some words
down in various places.

Gid washed his face and dried it with a towel, then
walked out of the kitchen over to the table.

"What you got there, Brad?"

"This is a map of the other caches. Before I came
here, I set up some along the way we'll go after we pick
up Randy and Lou. I got some information from army
scouts that tells me where Thorne has been and where
he's headed."

"Was he the one who burned my cotton fields?"

"Seems like."

"What's in that bundle?"

"Unwrap it."

"I see that box of .44 cartridges. For the Spencer?"

"Fits both the Colt and the rifle," Brad said.

Gid picked up the bundle and unwrapped it. He whistled when he saw the new Colt .44.

"I cleaned the grease out of it," Brad said. "You might want to rub that oil off."

"That's a mighty fine pistol," Gid said as he hefted it and held it out at arm's length. "Good balance."

"You hit a man in his little finger and it'll knock him down."

"I guess you might be ready to ride out about now."

"As soon as we can. We've got some daylight to burn."

"I'll get my holster and see if this .44 fits it."

"There are U.S. Army holsters in the cache if it doesn't."

"You thought of everything, didn't you, Brad?"

"I tried to."

Gid went into the other room carrying the pistol. He emerged a few minutes later with his gunbelt strapped on and the Colt jutting nicely from it. Under his left arm, he carried his bedroll. He now wore a Confederate cap, as well. His hair stuck out from under it like dark spikes.

"About the same size as my own cap and ball," Gid said.

"You could use a haircut, Gid."

"I'll chop at it now and then."

Brad stood up. He started for the door. When he reached it, he looked back. Gid was still standing there as if glued to the floor.

And he was shaking like a willow tree in a windstorm.

7

GID STOOD THERE, TRANSFIXED, HIS EYES GLAZED OVER
with a wet film, his body trembling in every muscle. For
a moment, Brad thought he might be about to go into a
fit. Gid's mouth was open and his lips were quivering
as if he might be freezing to death right in the middle
of a Texas summer.

"Gid, what's wrong?"

Gid's eyes closed and he did not open them for several moments.

*He was scared. He knew that. He had been scared
ever since they left Fort Brown. He had never killed a
man before and no man had ever shot at him, white or
red. He hoped it didn't show. He didn't want the other
men to know that he felt as if he had a dull knife in his
gut that was slowly twisting it into knots, and he had to
make fists of his hands so that his fingers would not
tremble.*

*The other men seemed eager, and so did the cavalry
horses. Captain Chambers kept the column moving so
that the horses had to step out. His own horse seemed
to sense his fear; the big bay mare had been skittery
ever since they left the fort and it was all he could do*

to keep it from prancing right on out of ranks. The horse's name was Jenny, and she was four years old, but acted like a frisky colt that day. And Gid's gut kept tightening with those knots until he thought he might lose his breakfast grub.

From what he'd heard, they had to ride almost to Laredo, to someplace called Zapata, named after some damned Mex bandit. The Rio Grande was blinding him with its light as the sun struck it and turned it into a ribbon of muddy water with every ripple and wave glinting like mirrors. The Mexicans still called it the Rio Bravo here in the south and only called it the Rio Grande someplace up north, maybe around Santa Fe. Stupid Mexicans. Now there was this Ochoa, who was a damned bandit and wanted control over the Rio from Brownsville to Laredo as if it were his personal property. More likely he wanted to rob people who traveled this infernal road.

"Corporal Tunstal, report to Captain Chambers. On the double."

He hadn't seen the rider come up on his right and he was still blinded by the river when he turned to look.

"Me?"

"You're Gideon Tunstal, aren't ye?"

"Yes."

"Cap'n wants to see you. Follow me."

He followed the private's galloping horse up to the front of the column. The private, a man named Ned Corby, saluted Captain Chambers and turned his horse in a tight circle to rejoin the column next to the guidon carrier.

"Gid, I got a job for you," Chambers said.

"You want me to ride back to the fort with a message, Captain?"

"Don't you just wish. Listen. We've got Ochoa spotted. Lou just rode back and Randy's gone on ahead to keep an eye on the Mexicans. From what Lou tells me, we have a chance to catch them by surprise."

"What is it you want me to do, Brad . . . I mean, Cap'n?"

"Take a dozen men from the rear and ride out about two hundred yards on my right flank. Keep me in sight and watch for my signal. You're going to act like a scorpion's tail, son."

"What?"

"A scorpion's tail. When I give you the high sign, I want you to ride like hell and close up an arc at the river and flank Ochoa. We'll come in from this side."

"You think twelve men are enough?"

"I think you're the best shot in this outfit, Gid, and you know who the others are. You take them with you. Lou says Ochoa's camped at a ford and I don't want him to go anyplace but across that river back into Mexico. And I want him to pay dearly for the privilege. Now, can you handle this assignment?"

"I reckon, sir."

"Damn it, Gid, I know you're scared purple. So am I. So is everyone in my troop. Now, get your ass back there and pick some men. We'll be on Ochoa in a half hour or so."

"That soon?"

"Gid, go on, now. I'm counting on you to act as my pincer."

"Sir, I don't know nothin' about tactics, 'cept what they taught us."

"It'll all become clear to you once you hear our rifles cracking."

"Yes, sir."

"Don't worry about a thing, Gid. That fear will go away once you get into the thick of battle."

Brad strode over to Gid and placed his hands on the man's shoulders. "Gid, snap out of it."

Gid opened his eyes. As suddenly as he did, he stopped shaking and his eyes cleared after a moment.

"Sorry, Brad. When . . . I mean . . . I keep thinking about . . . aw, nothin'. I'm all right."

"Before I forget it, I made a map of those caches. In case anything happens."

"Anything happens? What do you mean?"

"I mean in case we get separated, or you need to re-supply."

"You mean if you get killed."

"I mean just in case, Gid. Snap out of it. We've got some riding to do."

"I've got to catch up my horse."

"I can do that for you. Where's he pastured?"

"I've got a half dozen in the north pasture. About a half mile from here."

"Saddle?"

"You'll have to bring him back here. But I'll go with you if your horse packs double."

"He does. Let's go."

Forty-five minutes later, the two men were riding toward Lou Reeves's place. Gid was riding a big bay mare, a six-year-old that seemed to have good bottom and good chest. She bore a CSA brand on her rump and stood fifteen hands high. Brad remembered the horse. Gid called her Jenny and he had ridden her the day they chased Ochoa across the border back into Mexico.

Randy came riding back to the column in a hurry. His horse was sleek with sweat and his uniform was stained with his own perspiration.

"Cap'n, the Mexes got wind of us," Randy said, panting. "We got to get after 'em right now."

"Did you see Gid's column?"

"I saw him. They're ridin' in to fight right now."

"Good. Rest your horse, Randy. Stay behind and walk him, cool him down. He's about to start lathering."

"But . . ."

"That's an order, Sergeant."

"Yes, sir."

The column broke into a gallop. He looked back and waved to break up the formation. The riders fanned out until they were riding a wedge.

The crack of rifles peppered the air with popping sounds. Close. He drew his rifle from its scabbard and nodded to his lieutenant, who signaled the order to the other cavalrymen. He pointed to the bugler, who sounded the charge.

Puffs of smoke appeared over the rise as the cavalry troop swarmed onto the field of battle. Mexicans swimming in the shallows of the river began streaking for the opposite shore. Horses in the Ochoa camp shrieked and whinnied as men scrambled to catch them, knocking over kettles and scattering fires. Some of the men were shooting into the air or at dubious targets.

Gid's troop swarmed to the attack as Brad's men entered the fray from the opposite direction. Women screamed and some Mexicans ran on foot to the river, while others, mounted, ran in circles, with bullets whistling around them and kicking up dirt and dust when they missed a moving target.

A mass of Mexicans on small, fleet horses waded into the river, heading for the Mexican side. Gid shot a man out of the saddle who was riding toward him firing two pistols, his reins clamped between his teeth.

Brad sent part of his troops to the right in an encircling movement, and five Mexicans who were riding for the open plain turned their horses and galloped toward the river. Brad shot one of them off a bareback horse and saw him hit the ground and skid a dozen feet, leaving a streak of blood on the ground.

A Confederate trooper grunted and cried out as a ball struck him in the leg. Another trooper shot the Mexican who had drawn blood as he turned to run on foot toward his confused horse.

Puffs of white smoke blossomed over the Mexican camp and some of those who had reached the other side began firing on Gid and his men. Brad yelled to his men as he charged toward the river. "Chase 'em across and keep going."

The fighting turned savage as riders from both sides

crossed and recrossed moving lines that wavered and
opened and reclosed. A thick cloud of dust arose from
the earth as the running horses tore up the ground with
their hooves. Smoke and dust obscured some of the fight-
ers, and some of the shooting was at point-blank range
as combatants met like jousting knights at close quar-
ters. Men threw up their hands as bullets and ball ripped
through them, and the wounded fell among the dead with
the acrid smell of burnt powder and spilled blood in
their nostrils.

Finally, the Mexicans began to stream across the
river, shooting their rifles and pistols as they waded the
ford, and some of these were cut down and their horses
foundered with wounds that knocked them over, their
hides streaked with blood. Men floated facedown in the
current, while others flailed in the bloody waters and
were washed downstream before drowning or succumb-
ing to their injuries.

There were moments of chaos and confusion as the
Confederates all converged on the retreating Mexicans,
and then Gid and his men crossed the river and began
chasing the fleeing enemy, sounding rebel yells of exultation as the dust spooled out behind the Mexican
horses at the gallop.

Brad moved his men across the river and they shot
down Mexican stragglers and merged with Gid and his
men to form a band of cavalry in full chase, out of formation, yelling insults in raspy voices as if they were at
a steeplechase following the hounds in full cry after the
fox.

Brad held his men up as the distance widened between
his troopers and the escaping Mexicans.

"That's good enough," he yelled. And motioned to
Gid to turn his men back.

The troopers reined up their horses and turned them.
Sergeants and corporals called for order and formation.
They passed wounded and dying men and those already
gone. The faces of the troopers were drawn and tight

and covered with dust and the peppering of black powder and red pips from burning blowback.

They crossed back to the American side of the Rio Grande and fell into parade formation. Brad ordered a count of the dead and beckoned to Gid, who rode over and saluted.

"You did well, Gid."

"Thank you, sir."

"I notice your hands are steady."

"Yes, sir, I'm—I mean—I don't get the shakes once the battle starts. It's just right before. And I ain't scared none, it's just somethin'. Like buck fever."

"You don't have to explain it to me, Gid. I'm promoting you to sergeant. Sew your stripes on when we get back to the fort."

"Yes, sir. And, thanks, Brad. Sir."

Brad laughed and slapped Gid on the back as he turned his horse.

They counted twenty dead Mexicans that day and no cavalry fatalities. Ochoa had gotten away, but he never returned to the U.S. side of the border for the remainder of the war.

Colonel John Salmon Ford was pleased with the results of that first engagement of the Civil War.

And so was Brad Chambers, along with his newly promoted sergeant, Gideon Tunstal.

They crossed the Laguna Salado early in the afternoon when the sun was still high in the sky. It was bleak country, with traces of salt grass barely hanging on to the soil, a treeless plain seemingly devoid of life except for the wheeling buzzards circling under a canopy of pale blue sky and the occasional hawk that floated overhead on silent pinions.

They skirted around lands of the Falfurrias Ranch and threaded their way westward and left long lean shadows in their wake. Brad kept looking over his shoulder every time he thought he saw something and there were times when he thought he saw, through the shimmers of heat rising from the puddles of mirages, a far-off rider or two dogging their trail. But he shook off the feeling, believing that he was only seeing things that were not there, like the small lakes glinting in the slant of the burning afternoon sun.

Ahead, though, Gid pointed to a column of smoke, like a child's charcoal scrawl, hanging in the sky, black and ominous as if it were some marker placed there to warn them to go back whence they came.

"What do you make of it, Brad?" Gid asked.

"Mighty odd."

"Do you know what lies yonder?"

"A line shack, maybe a ranch house. Hard to remember, it's been so long since I rode this way."

"That ain't Lou's place, is it?"

"No, but it's mighty close. Seems to me I recollect being there once or twice, beyond the Falfurrias spread."

"I been there. Was some adobes over yonder, Mexicans living in them."

"Yeah, I think I know a Mexican who came from these parts. Used to buy cattle from him and we caught horses over the border and run them back to my place."

"Me, too. Gallegos."

"That's the man. Francisco Gallegos. That was a long time ago."

"You called him Paco, I think."

"Yeah, Paco," Brad said, and his abdomen tightened. He looked up at the sky and saw the buzzards floating toward the smoke and he smelled something on the wind, like cooked meat, like beef, he thought, and his stomach muscles began to quiver.

Brad looked over his shoulder when he thought he saw the shadow following him, but there was nothing to be seen for a thousand yards or more.

And then, they began to see signs that something was wrong. A longhorn steer lay next to a stock tank, stiff as a chunk of shale, a bullet hole in its head, just under the boss. They began to see more dead cattle and then

they saw the ruins of an adobe house, its thatched roof
still smoldering, and beyond, a barn still afire, sending
up the column of smoke, and all around it, dead horses
and cattle, as if a wind of death had blown through and
lay waste to all in its path.

"I remember this place now," Brad said, a somber
tone to his voice. "This was where Paco Gallegos lived."

"And not far beyond it is Randy's spread," Gid said.

"Whatever happened here, happened just today."

"Looks like, Brad."

They rode up to the adobe, with its roof gone, its
insides gutted by fire. In the soundless space between
the adobe and the barn, there lay three dead dogs and a
wiry-haired cat.

Just then, both men ducked as they heard the crack
of a rifle. They both heard the sizzle of a bullet as it
fried the air over their heads.

Brad jerked his rifle from its scabbard and flattened
himself atop his horse. Gid dismounted and pushed his
horse down as it had been trained to do, jerking his rifle
free.

For a long moment, neither man heard anything. It
was as if time had suddenly stood still.

8

BRAD HUGGED THE GROUND AND BEGAN TO SLITHER sideways toward Gid, who was hidden behind his downed horse, looking toward the trees where the shots had come from.

"See anything?" Gid asked.

"Nary," Brad answered.

"Shots came from those trees yonder."

"I know. I don't think whoever fired at us was trying to kill us."

Brad moved his rifle closer to Gid, then edged his body over toward the rifle, inch by inch, expecting another round to be shot off at any second.

He froze a moment later, when they both heard something move. The two men ducked when they heard a twig snap.

"*Quién es?*"

The voice came from the trees.

"That's a Mexican," Gid whispered.

"I know." Then Brad said, "*Amigos. Somos amigos. Me llamo Chambers.*"

A long moment of silence.

"Chambers?" Mexican accent.

"Brad Chambers."

"Brad? Is that you, *verdad*?"

"Who in hell is it?" Gid asked.

"Sounds like Paco. Wait," Brad replied.

"Paco? Is that you? Come on out. It's me, Brad Chambers. *De los caballos, recuerdes*?"

"Yes, yes. The horses. *Esperate*. Wait. I am coming."

Brad's palms were sweating. He had not heard Paco's voice in a long time. He was trying hard to remember it as he waited.

They crossed the Rio Grande after midnight, their horses making the moon's shining spangles rumple and winkle, and he knew it was a bad night because the moon was full, but Paco knew where the horses were and the animals would not wait until the moon waned. The river was shallow at that place, but swift, and his horse struggled against the current and he listened to the burble of the water around their horses' legs and it sounded like the muffled plucking of a guitar or a harp. They reached the opposite shore and the horses shook themselves and switched their tails and below the girth straps, their legs glistened in the soft light of the moon and they seemed like magical steeds, part silver, part hide and bone.

Paco pointed and led out and Brad followed his Mexican friend along some dim trail that he could not see clearly, but knew was there. The wet shod hooves did not make much noise on the ground for a time and he was glad of that, because on such a night every little sound carried a long way, maybe for miles across the pewtered desert with its empty silence like the silence of an immense hall or a church with the star-sprinkled sky for a roof and the Milky Way spangling the dark like the moon on the river. It seemed, for a time, that he and his horse were part of another world that was not real, but belonged to the sky and the night and the whispering river behind them.

Paco did not speak and they rode on through the

trackless plain like wraiths, voiceless and without faces or names, and the land changed and they skirted deep arroyos and lancing cholla and treacherous nopales— the prickly pear—and the things of the desert took on ominous shapes. His senses prickled and danced as he rode through the strange, unknown world of the night with the stars so far away and cold and winking like wise eyes peeking through a black shroud and the moon shining now so bright he could not look at it directly else he turn eyeless and blind.

Paco, a black shape against the black land, a centaur emerged from the mists of time, ahead of him, leading the way, the twisting, turning, cautious way, until the lanterns appeared in the distance, like fireflies flickering in a cactus garden, and then, looming larger until he thought they could be fallen stars turned to gold. Then he could see the jacales and smell the horses, smell the piss and dung and smoldering hides of them and before the horses in the rope corrals could whicker, Paco stopped and he rode up to him and waited, too, for a time. They dismounted and hunkered down behind a cactus-strewn hillock and lit the cigarettes they rolled and listened to the night sounds and waited without speaking as their own horses scrabbled for grass on the sparse landscape. The moon slid down the arc of the vaulted heavens and when they looked again, the lanterns had gone dark. They started walking toward the little village, leading their horses, holding their muzzles so that they would not give warning with their whinnies and when they saw the horses finally, Paco stopped again and they mounted up and drew their knives, which were honed to a surgical sharpness. They nodded to each other and separated to encircle the rope corral and converge on it from opposite directions.

They kept their horses to a slow walk and it seemed to him that it took hours to get to that place where he would launch his charge, and by then he could see the Mexican vaqueros asleep around the embers of their campfire and smell the mezcal on their breaths as they breathed. When he saw Paco raise his arm, Brad jabbed the rowels of his spurs into his horse's flanks and felt the wind blow on his face, the wind that had not been there before but was now generated by the running horse. When he reached the ropes, he leaned down and slashed them with his knife. The ropes parted and the corral collapsed. He sheathed his knife and drew his cap and ball and fired into the sky, pushing the freed horses before him. The sleeping Mexicans awoke and yelled and cursed, and the horses scattered the coals of the fire and raced past the jacales and toward the river, with Paco on one flank and he on the other, both bent over their pommels as rifles cracked like broken dry sticks behind them and lead balls whined in the air like whistling doves in flight.

And the thunder of the hooves rose up around him and he felt pleasure race through him like the fire in his loins when he lay with his wife. He yelled at the horses and barked at those trying to break free of the pack and drove them back in to the galloping herd until there was just one rippling, surging throng racing with him, the moon on their backs like the glistening sheen on the river. When they slowed, finally, Paco turned to him and smiled and his smile shone brighter than the moon. They forded the river with horses docile from fatigue and as they reached the other side, his exultation was complete, his veins tingling as if he had drunk mezcal himself, filled his belly with the warm spirits brewed from the eternal plants that harbored the desert heat in their fibers and released them into his blood and brain in the form of liquid lightning.

And he knew then what it was like to be rich, to own the earth and the sky and the most beautiful horses in the world, all sleek and shining from the moon and wet from the river as if newly born by some arcane and magical process.

"It really you, *mi amigo*?" Paco said as he emerged

from the copse of live oaks and mesquite, carrying his old rifle. Brad looked at him intently. Paco did not seem to have changed much. He was a short, wiry man, with a sun-bronzed face, thick mustache, long sideburns, and sparse, thinning black hair. He did not seem to have aged much. Perhaps the lines in his face were a little deeper, the creases around the mouth slightly more pronounced. But Paco walked with a steady firm gait and he held his head proudly and his back was straight, as always.

Paco had never married, Brad knew, because he had grown up hating his father for beating his mother, and hating his mother for letting his father beat him. He trusted few men and no women at all.

"Yes, Paco. Me'n a friend." In Spanish he asked, "What passed here?"

"Do you not see? Look at what is written on the wall of my adobe."

Brad turned to the burned adobe and saw what had been scrawled on the wall with charcoal: GO BACK TO MEXICO OR DIE.

"Do you know who did this, Paco?" Brad asked as his friend walked up to them.

"No. It happened before the sun rose up this morning. I was outside taking the piss when they started shooting at my house. I ran and hid in the trees. They tried to kill me, I think, but they did not see me."

"Paco, this is Gideon Tunstal. He and I are hunting these men. They will hang for what they did to you."

"You should shoot them when you see them, Brad. They are bad men. They killed my cow, my pigs, and stole my horses. You remember my horses?"

"Yes, Paco," Brad said, "I remember your horses. We will try and get them back for you."

Brad looked at the ruins of Paco's place. The lean-to barn was still standing; the outhouse had not been damaged, but the hog pens were full of carcasses, and a pair of goats lay sprawled next to a stock tank, shot dead. What kind of man could perform such senseless acts,

Brad wondered, but even as he asked himself that question, he knew. Abel Thorne. And there were men like him in every society. Perhaps he had learned such things from the Comanches. Or perhaps Thorne had taught them their devilish ways.

"Come, I will see if I can find some coffee inside my house and a pot. I have the well and the pump and I know where I can get a horse."

"Why do you want a horse?" Brad asked.

"Because, when you go after those men, I am going with you."

Gid and Brad exchanged glances that Paco did not see. He was already walking toward the burned-out hulk of his little adobe and, for a man his age, he had a surprising spring in his step.

9

Brad and Gid waited for Paco while he rummaged around inside his smoldering adobe. They built smokes and sat on the ground, listening to Paco banging around inside the *casita*.

"I can't figure this Thorne out," Gid said. "What in hell does he want, anyway?"

"Abel Thorne was a drifter before the war. Up from N'Orleans, I reckon, or so they said. He worked for me at roundup a time or two, vaqueroed for some other ranchers. Worked on the King, at Falfurrias, finally got enough money scrabbled together to buy him a small spread. Claimed he once knew the Bowie brothers, helped Jim and his brother smuggle Negro slaves out of N'Orleans."

"Was that true?"

"I don't know. But he had him some slaves; raised cotton and did some farming, had a few head of mixed-breed cattle. I saw one or two of 'em once, and they looked like they'd been ironed."

"Ironed?"

"Brands changed with a running iron."

"Oh. A damned cattle rustler."

"Nobody ever proved anything. I heard he shot a man who called him out about some suspicious cattle up in Abilene, but there were always rumors floating around this part of the country."

"Especially just before the war broke out," Gid said.

"Yeah. Thorne shot off his mouth over to Kingsville about the right to own slaves and I guess nobody paid him much attention. Turned out, he was smuggling slaves up from Galveston and Corpus Christi, takin' 'em up north and lining his pockets pretty damned good."

"So, Thorne was not only a slave holder, but smuggling 'em in and sellin' 'em. A damned slave trader."

"I reckon. I heard more about him after I joined the Texas Rangers. The Rangers had orders to bring him in for smuggling contraband and Rip Ford picked me, Randy, and Lou to go after him."

"You never told me that," Gid said.

"Forgot all about it. Before we could go after him, I joined the Union army and figured old Rip would take Thorne down. I guess he didn't get the chance."

"War broke out before he could."

"We were all running around like chickens with our heads cut off. We never thought Texas would secede. Sam Houston argued against it. Then he retired and moved to Corpus Christi and those old boys up in Austin voted to secede from the Union. Caught a bunch of us plumb by surprise."

"Yeah, me too."

"Well, it's all water under the bridge now. Except that Thorne, it seems like, carries one hell of a big grudge around with him."

"The bastard."

Paco emerged from the gutted adobe, a look of chagrin on his face. He was carrying a battered old coffee pot that was burnt to a crisp. He was trying to rub off the soot, but not making much progress.

"That pot's got a hole in it, Paco," Brad said. "Hold it up and take a look."

Paco lifted the pot, saw that there was a small hole on the bottom rim. He looked crestfallen just before he hurled the pot high into the air and watched it tumble to the ground.

"I found a handful of coffee, too," Paco said, patting one of his shirt pockets.

"No importa," Brad said, putting out his quirly. "We ought to get after those boys, anyhow. You said you had a horse to ride?"

"Yes, I think so. Last night, one of the horses, she ran off and I could not catch her."

"Do you know where this horse is?" Brad asked.

"I think she runs to the creek. She always does that when I am not looking."

"How far?" Gid asked.

"I do not know. A mile, maybe. Maybe two. Maybe three."

Gid swore. Brad laughed.

"I can pack double," Brad said.

"It is not far, I think," Paco said. "The creek, she is not much far. Wait, I will get the bridle."

Paco ran over to the lean-to on spindly legs and disappeared in the shadows. He emerged a few seconds later, carrying an old worn leather bridle with a worn, thin bit. He climbed up behind Brad. "Let us go," he said.

Once mounted behind Brad, Paco pointed the way and the three men rode toward the creek.

"We'll want to get on those tracks, Gid, while they're fresh."

"I could maybe follow them a ways and you could catch up with me," Gid said.

"We probably shouldn't split up."

"Whatever you say, Brad."

"They'll keep until we catch up Paco's horse. You have a saddle, Paco?"

"I sold the saddle last week for some food."

"You must be having a bad time," Brad said.

"No," Paco said. "It was my stomach that was having the bad time."

Gid and Brad laughed, but Brad felt a pang of sorrow for how things were going for his old friend. It seemed to him that the war had been hard on everyone in Texas, perhaps in the nation. And apparently the suffering was not over. As long as men like Abel Thorne still harbored hatred and sought revenge for what fate had handed them, the war would continue to cause hardship for many people.

The horse stood hipshot in the shade of a scrimpy willow shading a bend in the creek with its drooping branches and thin leaves. The horse did not move when Brad and Gid rode up to it. It did not even whicker at the other horses, both of which eyed it warily.

"Not much of a horse," Gid said.

"To me, he is beautiful," Paco said, sliding down the rump of Brad's horse, releasing his grip on the cantle just before his feet touched the ground.

The horse was a gelding. Its pale sorrel hide looked moth-eaten, with several scabbed-over sores on its chest, flanks, and legs. Streaks of blood marked the recent fly bites it had suffered. Its ribs stood outlined against the hide like barrel slats and there was a distinct sway to its back.

"I don't think that sorry horse could make ten miles with Paco on its back," Gid said.

"Oh, no, he is a strong horse," Paco said, grinning. *"Muy fuerte."*

"I've got some grain in one of my saddlebags," Brad said.

"He does not need the grain," Paco said, slipping the bridle on the stolid horse, pressing the bit between its worn-down teeth. "He eats the *nopal* when I cut the spines off, and the salt grass."

"He don't look like he's eaten much lately," Gid said.

"Maybe he would like a little grain," Paco said, taking off his hat and holding it out upside down.

Brad climbed down out of the saddle, untied his bedroll, and removed his saddlebags. He poured two handfuls of oats mixed with dried corn into Paco's hat. "See if he'll eat this, Paco."

Paco took his hat over to his horse and held it under the horse's muzzle. The horse sniffed and blinked. Then it switched its tail and scattered two of the blood-sucking flies on its rump. It poked its mouth inside the hat and worried the grain around before starting to take some into its mouth and grinding away at it.

"That horse is plumb starved," Gid said. "Look at it."

"I think he is a little hungry," Paco said.

Brad said nothing. He felt his gut tighten with the sadness of it. Paco was starving. His horse was starving. And some bastard had come along and killed his goats and hogs and burned down his house. He was beginning to hate Abel Thorne and he had never really hated anyone before. Not anyone he knew by name, anyway, and even that one time, it had only been for a little while. He had hated hard, then, but the hate had gone away, he thought, forever, when he heard a few simple words that were never even spoken aloud.

She must have known he would be hurt. She must have known that even before she betrayed him, but he could not tell by looking at her face. She had been crying and the tears were still wet on her swollen face. And that hurt him, too. Way down deep.

"Brad, I'm sorry," Mary said. "I didn't mean it to go that far. I didn't want to hurt you."

"You did hurt me. You hurt me now."

She reached over to touch his arm, but he pulled away from her and she drew back and that hurt him, too. To treat her like that. To be so cruel. To be as cruel as she had been to him.

"Brad, I'm trying to apologize. I'm trying to make up to you. Is it going to be this way?"

"Mary, I've got to know. Who was it?"

"I'm not going to tell you, Brad."

"Why?"

"Because I'm afraid of what you might do."

"I'm not going to do anything. I just want to know who it was you took to our bed while I was gone."

"That would do no good. To tell you."

"Yes, it would."

"You might do something we'll both regret," she said.

"I still want to know. You owe me that much."

"No, please, Brad. I don't want you to know. It—it just happened, that's all. I—I don't love him."

"You must have had some feelings for the man. There must have been some reason you did this to me."

"Brad, I didn't do it to you. I did it to myself, and I'm deeply sorry. Can't you just accept that?"

"No. I want the name of the man."

Again, she reached out for him, but he drew away once more and found that he could not look at her, could not look into her smoky eyes, could not look at the tears welling up in them. It was as if he were afraid he might see someone else in her eyes besides himself.

"Is it going to be this way, then, Brad? Are you going to draw a line in this house, in our bed, that I dare not cross?"

"Damn it, Mary, I want to know who you did it with, and for how long you've been cuckolding me."

"No good would come of my telling you about it. Brad, I don't love the man. I didn't at the time. I was lonely. He passed by and was flattering to me. I let things get out of hand. He's not in our life now and he never will be."

"Mary, you'll force me to look into the face of every man I meet and wonder if he was the one. I won't be able to trust anyone I know."

"It isn't anyone you know, Brad. And you'll never meet him."

"How can you say that?"

"I know. He doesn't live around here and he'll never come back."

"How long was he here?"

"A week."

"A week. Well, I guess he had a high old time, the bastard."

"Brad, please."

"I want to know the son-of-a-bitch's name, Mary. Now."

She got up from the bed where they were sitting and walked to the window. He knew she was crying. He could see her shoulders shaking. But she made no sound and that made it worse for him. She was tearing him apart inside. He couldn't stand to see a woman cry and now he was beginning to feel as if he were the one who was at fault.

"Brad, I'm sorry. That's all I can say." She turned to him and touched the tears on her face, wiped them away. She looked so sad, he thought. Wasn't that punishment enough? Did he even want to punish her for her unfaithfulness? He did not know. He was confused and angry. Yet his heart went out to her, for some reason he could not explain.

"I know you're sorry, Mary. I'm sorry, too. I wish you hadn't done this to us, to me. I wish none of it had ever happened."

"So do I."

The man had left his pipe and tobacco pouch behind and Brad had found it when he returned from a long trip to San Angelo. And the man's tobacco smoke still reeked in the house. He had confronted her, and she had lied at first, then broken down and admitted her infidelity.

"I'm not ever going to say his name again," she said. "Not to you, not to anyone. It's something I'll have to bear, a shame I'll have to carry in my heart all my days, Brad. Please don't press me any further. I'm terribly sorry and it will never happen again."

"I don't trust you anymore, Mary."

She rushed to him then, the tears welling up in her

*broken eyes and pouring down her cheeks, and she knelt
down in front of him and buried her head in his lap and
kept sobbing, her body shaking, her weeping ripping him
asunder as if someone were driving knives into his heart,
into his soul.*

"Mary, please. Don't cry. Please, God, don't cry."

*She stopped sobbing for a moment and lifted her
head. He looked down into her eyes and it seemed to
him they swirled with sorrow and pain and he touched
her soft hair and then dug his fingers in and began
kneading her scalp and she closed her eyes and her lips
moved soundlessly.*

*"I love you." Her mouth formed the unspoken words
that shot into his heart. And all the hate went out of him
in that moment and he lifted her up and took her into
his arms and held her fast until she stopped trembling.*

"I love you too, Mary."

"Let's get to those tracks," Brad said abruptly, shaking himself out of his reverie.

Gid looked at him with an odd expression on his face.

"Yes, sir," Gid said, a tone of mocking respect in his
voice.

"If you salute me, I'll knock you on your ass, Gid,"
Brad said as he climbed back into the saddle. He started
riding back to the place where they would start tracking
and he did not look back.

That was the bad thing about hatred, he thought. It
was liable to lash out at anyone, at any time. It was not
a good thing to carry around for very long. He could
already feel his hatred for Abel Thorne beginning to eat
away at him like one of those worms that got inside a
man's belly and devoured his innards so slowly that he
never even felt it until it was too damned late.

<u>10</u>

BRAD STUDIED THE TRACKS HEADING WESTWARD FROM
Paco's ruined farm. Gid looked on, counting on his fingers.

"I make out six riders," Gid said.

"I'd say five," Brad said.

"I counted six sets of tracks. What did you come up with?"

"There are six shod horses, all right. Or maybe five horses and a mule."

"How do you figure that?" Gid asked.

Paco grinned and pointed to one set of tracks. "This one carries much weight," he said.

"Huh?" Gid grunted.

"I figure they're pulling a pack horse. Five riders, one pack horse. Or mule."

"By damn, I think you're right," Gid said. "Unless one horse is packing double."

"We'll know in a while," Brad said. "If the weight shifts too much, the tracks will show it. So, if one horse is packing double, the tracks will show us that."

"You've got eyes like an eagle, Brad," Gid said.

"I learned tracking from the best," Brad said. "My first

time out as a Ranger, I rode with a crackerjack tracker, Bobby Wakefield. He told me he learned how to track from an old Kickapoo when he was a boy."

"Well, I reckon we'll see soon enough if we're trailin' five men or seven," Gid said.

"I make it five," Brad said. "Let's see where these tracks take us. Looks to me like they're heading right where I want to go."

"You mean to pick up Reeves and Dunn," Gid said.

"Yep. I'll lead out. Paco, you bring up the rear and keep looking over your shoulder. Gid, you watch our flanks."

"For what?" Gid asked.

"Any one of those riders could double back on us. You keep a sharp lookout, hear?"

"Yes, sir," Gid said, in that same mocking tone he had used before.

Brad concealed his annoyance by turning his head and ticking his horse in the flanks. The three men rode alongside the tracks as Brad followed them, putting together a picture in his mind about the men who had raided Paco's place and the mounts they rode.

The little boy was still shaking two days after it happened. His clothes were dirty and his face was still smeared where he had wiped away his tears. He was very thin and his hair was uncombed. His eyes, though, dark and darting, burned like two black coals when he told them what had happened.

"They come up on my pa," the boy said, "over yonder where he was pullin' up a stump with our old mule. They snuck up on him and I seen one of 'em cut his head nigh clean off with a long knife. I was in the barn yonder, playin', and I seen it plain. Then, they all come up to the house and next thing I know, they was a-draggin' my ma outside and they tore off all her clothes and . . ."

"Son, you don't have to tell all of it," Bobby Wakefield said. "We know they killed your ma, too. What's your name?"

"*Jimmy Don Clark. Junior.*"

"*What all did they take, Jimmy Don?*" Bobby asked the boy.

"*They took two milk cows and my pet goat, and our horse. They rode off yonder.*" The boy pointed to the northwest.

"*I'm real sorry about your ma and pa,*" Bobby said. "*I'll say a prayer for them.*"

"*My aunt says they went to heaven.*"

Bobby looked at the boy's aunt, who was standing with her husband several yards away. Their son was sitting on the porch of Jimmy Don's empty house. He was the one who had told the Rangers about the Apache raid, riding half a day to get to Fort Worth, and then back again without sleeping.

"*You go with your aunt and uncle now, Jimmy Don,*" Wakefield said. "*Me'n Brad here are going to hunt down those Apaches.*"

"*Are you going to kill them?*" the boy asked.

"*We'll give 'em a chance to surrender peaceably.*"

"*I hope you kill them.*"

"*We'll see to it that they are brought to justice, son. One way or another.*"

"*Yes, sir,*" the boy said, and they left him with his kin and rode off, but he could not forget that haunted look in the boy's eyes and that last request of his before they took up the trail of the marauding Apaches.

"*We'll never find them, Bobby. They've got a two-day head start on us and the wind's blown away their tracks, more'n likely.*"

"*Brad,*" Bobby said, "*when a man goes somewhere, no matter where, he leaves some kind of track. And it don't matter none if the wind blows or the rain washes 'em away, there's always a trace, some sign of where he passed.*"

"*I don't see how, Bobby.*"

"*Two days isn't much of a start if you know what to look for. I'll teach you how to follow a track as we go,*" *and you'll know as much as I do. I'll teach you, just like an old Kickapoo taught me."*

"How'd he do that?"

"He told me to study the ground carefully and then tell him what I saw."

"And what did you tell him you saw?"

"I saw two ants carrying a seed across that little piece of ground. They would stop to rest and pick it up again. What's more, I saw their tracks, ever so faint, and the impression of the seed when they put it down. I saw a doodlebug make its tracks on its way to a patch of sand. I saw a young lizard cross and leave its tracks. I saw steam rising from the ground as the sun came up and I watched the soil dry out and saw what that did to the little bitty tracks. Oh, I saw a lot of things, but he said I did not see enough and said I did not see everything."

"So, what did you do?"

"He made me go back the next day and look at that same patch of ground. In fact, I looked at it for a whole week and I saw what this old Kickapoo meant."

"What was that?"

"I saw life beneath the soil, saw sand fleas and mites and what they did, how they burrowed and what marks they left there."

"Sounds dumb to me."

"No, Brad, it wasn't dumb. I learned a lot in that week. I learned how to observe, to really see a track and into it and beyond it. And, when we, the Kickapoo and I, rode somewheres I always looked at the ground and he would make me tell him the story of the tracks whenever we saw any."

"And, can you tell me the story of these Apache tracks, Bobby?"

"I can and I will, as we go along."

The Apaches took pains to cover up their trail, but Bobby was smart enough to figure it out. The Indians rode over hard, flat ground at every opportunity and they used mesquite branches they tore off to brush away their tracks.

"They tied leafy branches to their horses' tails," Bobby said, "dragging them over their tracks. But those are tracks, too."

"Hard to see, though."

"Once you figure out what they're doing, it's not so hard."

"The tracks don't look very fresh, Bobby."

"Every once in a while, I'm seeing part of a hoof mark and I've seen enough now to know that one of their ponies has an injured hoof, there's a big chunk tore out of it, and another one's right forefoot needs trimming. It's starting to splay out and that leaves a distinctive mark on the ground. See. There."

"It almost looks like that was brushed over by the mesquite leaves."

"Similar, but not the same. That's slowing the horse some, and the loose hoof material is making an arcing swath inward. See?"

"I can see it now."

"It's the same every time I see it. That pony's trying to wear its hoof down."

"Kind of like trimming it itself."

"Yeah, just trying to rub off that little flap of hoof."

Wakefield seemed in no hurry, but he kept on the trail. "We're gaining on them," he said, "because they're trying to hide their tracks."

"Do they know we're tracking them?"

"I reckon they do," Bobby said.

They found the place where the Apaches had killed and butchered one of the milk cows. Bobby went over the ground carefully and, when he was finished, he said he knew how much they had eaten and how much beef they'd packed with them. Just by looking at the bones they left behind.

"They're packing what they can in the hide," Bobby

said. *"And now they're on the run. We'll catch up to
'em late tomorrow."*

"How do you know?"

*"They're no longer hiding their tracks, and pretty
soon they'll start leaving behind some of the stock they
took. I reckon they want to make it to the Pecos or the
Rio Grande pretty quick now."*

*The next morning, they found the other milk cow and
the goat, their dry tongues lolling from their mouths,
dead from the heat and the lack of water. Bobby kept
on going at a pretty good pace and by late afternoon,
the Apaches were waiting for them in a little draw, miles
from water.*

"Our canteens are full, Brad. We can wait 'em out."

"How long do you think that'll take?"

"In this dry, not long."

"Maybe they have full canteens, too."

*"I reckon not. None of 'em stopped to piss for the last
fifteen, twenty mile and that means they're dryin' up like
seed gourds."*

*The sun had scorched the earth for two days and what
moisture it didn't suck out of the ground, the West Texas
wind did and the Apaches hadn't gotten to any water in
four or five days by Bobby's figuring. Late in the afternoon, the Indians began chanting their death songs.*

"They know we're here, don't they, Bobby?"

"They do."

"Will they give up?"

"We'll see," he said.

*By late afternoon the sun was fairly boiling the blood
in a man's veins and one of the Apaches walked out
from the draw on wobbly legs.*

*When the others saw that they weren't going to be
shot, they walked out, too. Their horses were dead. They
had been drinking blood from their mounts and that only
made them thirstier.*

"They look pretty pathetic, Bobby."

"We'll get 'em to water tomorrow. By then, they ought to be right tame."

The wind came up late in the afternoon and blew sand and grit into their eyes and stung their faces raw. It was hell on the horses and hell on them and Brad called a halt well before the sun went down.

"No use going on until this wind dies down," he said.

"We'll lose Thorne's tracks," Gid said.

"Can't be helped. He'll have to get out of this, too. We may pick 'em up again tomorrow."

"I think they will get away," Paco said.

"They might," Brad said. "But wherever they go, they'll leave tracks and we'll find them."

"Do you think they'll go to Lou's or Randy's?"

"No. I don't think Thorne would pick on them. From what I've seen, he goes to places where he's unlikely to run into trouble."

"Like a coward," Gid said.

"Or somebody pretty smart."

"How long will we stay here?" Paco asked. "We will soon be buried in sand."

"Let's go on," Brad said. "It can't be much worse and maybe we'll ride on through it. The wind's blowing from the west."

"I'd rather ride than sit here and eat sand," Gid said.

The three men mounted up and rode into the brunt of the sandstorm like blind men plodding toward some uncharted oasis in the middle of a desert made almost invisible by the shrouding sand that filled the air and dimmed the light of the sun.

They rode on, bent to the wind, into the fading sunset, and Brad knew he had to find his way by dead reckoning. There was no sky, no landmark, no sign of life. There was only the ground beneath him, and it seemed to be moving as sheets of fine sand blew across the earth, blotting out all tracks, all that was known in the world, until finally, there was no longer any light as the sun set, and he could no longer see even the blowing, razoring sand that blistered his face, parched his lips and cracked them until they bled briefly before the sand cauterized them. Sand filled his nostrils and his mouth and throat and ears until he thought he would smother to death as the bleak, black night came on.

11

THE THREE RIDERS STUMBLED UP TO THE DOOR OF the ranch house, leading their horses for protection against the wind and the blowing sand. Brad had no idea what time it was, but he figured it was after midnight. The house was dark and he could barely recognize it.

"Hold my reins, Gid," he said, as he staggered up to the door.

"This where Reeves lives?" Gid asked.

Brad didn't answer. His throat was raw and he was trying hard to breathe. He pounded weakly on the door and pressed his ear against it to listen for any sounds from inside.

He heard nothing above the howling of the wind and his heart sank like a stone. He tried lifting the latch, but it was barred tight. Someone must be inside. He was too weak to call out, so he used both fists and pounded on the door again until the pain drove him to stop.

Again, Brad put his ear to the oaken door and tried to shut out the keening of the wind by clamping a hand over his other ear. He heard something then, or thought he did. A clumping sound. He slapped at the door with the open palm of his right hand. Another clump.

"Come on," he husked. "Come to the damned door, Lou."

He made a fist with his right hand and hammered a tattoo on the wall next to the door. Something rattled and then it was quiet. He pressed his ear tighter to the door. He jumped when he heard a voice on the other side.

"Who in hell are you, and what do you want?"

Brad recognized the voice. It was Reeves. He breathed a gasp of relief.

"Lou, it's Chambers. Open up."

"Brad?"

"Yes, damn it. Lift the latch, will you?"

"Just a damned minute."

Brad heard the bar lift and the latch rattle. The door opened and he barely made out the dim figure of Lou Reeves, looking like a ghost in his bleached long johns. He held a pistol in his hand and it was cocked.

"Are you going to let me in, Lou, or shoot me?"

"Christ, Brad. Come on in. Who's that with you?"

Brad lurched inside, out of the blistering wind. "Gid's with me and an old pard, Paco."

"I better help them put the horses up, then bring those boys in out of the wind. Christ, Brad, you look like you dug your way here underground. Want me to take the broom to you?"

"If you can get our horses put up, I'd be most obligated, Lou, and if you've a pail of water handy, point me to it."

"You going to drink it or pour it over you and make mud pies?"

"Very funny," Brad said. "Bring in my bedroll, saddlebags, and rifle, will you, Lou?"

"Water's in the kitchen, Major," Lou said. "Go easy on it, will you? I have to haul it in from the well."

Before Brad could lash Lou with a choice curse word, Lou was gone and the door slammed shut. He strode into the kitchen, glad to be out of the gale. He noticed that all the windows were covered with wet blankets and towels, soaked with water to absorb the sand that blew through every opening. There was only one lamp lit, in the front room, but light enough for him to see the buckets all over the kitchen. He found a pitcher and poured water into his mouth without bothering to look for a glass. The liquid soothed his parched throat. He swished the last mouthful around and spat into an empty basin. When he clamped his teeth together, he could still feel the sand and rinsed his mouth once more before going into the front room and falling into a leather chair, exhausted.

He stretched out his legs and felt the weariness seep through him. He hadn't realized how tired he was until he sat down. His eyes burned from the wind and there was sand in his ears and nostrils. He scraped some of it away and then closed his eyes to give them a rest. Outside, the wind keened like a banshee howling over an Irish bog and he wondered how they had made it this far, to shelter, in such a blow.

This night, he thought wryly, was truly not fit for man nor beast. It reminded him of another such windstorm, not long after he and Mary had been wed and he had brought his bride home, to live on his ranch. They had been happy, at first, but Mary was a city girl, and unused to the wild places, the long distances between neighbors, the seeming emptiness of a land that seemed to stretch forever and could, to her eyes, be bleak and harsh and cruel.

Mary was not prepared for the wind that came up that day. She had spent the morning planting seeds in their garden that spring. He was breaking a horse out in the corral, keeping an eye on the northwestern sky where the clouds had started to build, billowing up into great white thunderheads as the warm Gulf air surged up and crossed the Rio Grande, sped northward and westward into cooler air.

"Brad, look at the pretty clouds," Mary said, looking

up at the sky. "I've never seen a more beautiful day."

"Storm coming."

"Good. Maybe we'll get some rain on the seeds I've been planting."

"Might be some wind with that."

"The clouds seem to be moving very fast."

"Mary, I've got this horse gentled down. I'm going to throw a saddle on and take her for a ride."

"Be careful," she said.

The horse stood for the saddle, but the minute he boarded the mare, she bunched up her muscles and took off, straight-legged. The saddle turned into a hurricane deck as the horse twisted, fishtailed, humped, bucked, and tried to rub him off on one of the fenceposts and all of the rails. It was as if she had a burr under her blanket the way she contorted and whipped him this way and that, trying to unseat him. When she hit the ground, all four legs rigid as iron track, the shock ripped through his spine and rattled his brains.

"Brad," Mary called.

The mare ran around in circles, trying to escape, trying to toss him into the air, trying to flip him, but he stayed with her until he wore her out.

"Brad," Mary called again.

"Got her, Mary."

"No, look." She stood in the garden and pointed to the sky.

The white clouds were now coal-black and bulging with rain. They had moved closer and were coming on fast.

Then the wind hit and Mary screamed as her dress flapped and whipped and clung to her body. She leaned into the wind.

He led the horse into the barn and pushed her into a stall. He unsaddled her quickly as the wind rattled the door and made the walls quake. He had no time to rub the mare down, but went outside, bolted the barn door shut, and looked toward the garden. Mary leaned into *the gusting wind, turned, and then pitched headlong to the ground as a mighty blast of air struck her backside.*

He ran to her, picked her up. By then, the wind was roaring at them, a stiff, straight-line wind that almost made his knees buckle. He struggled with her to the house. It took him three or four minutes to get the door open. He shoved Mary inside and then put his shoulder down as the door tried to slam shut. Inside, he bolted the door and led Mary to the divan in the front room.

"This'll be the safest place."

"What is it?" she asked, her voice laden with bewilderment. "What's happening?"

"A big blow. We'll be all right."

"Brad, I'm scared."

"Don't worry. I'll be right here. Just got some things to do."

The house shook violently as the hard winds hit it and when he looked out the window, all he could see was dust in the air, moving toward them like a gigantic twister. In seconds, the garden, the fields, the corral and the barn, and the outhouse were all obscured by the blowing dust.

He hung blankets over the windows, but had no water to dampen them. The house began to fill with pulverized earth and grit and dust. Dust seeped in under the door and through every opening. The air inside was thick with it and Mary began to cough, struggling for breath.

He crammed sheets and blankets under both the front and back doors to try to keep out the blasting dust. The blankets helped some, but the winds increased in velocity and the house was pummeled by ferocious blasts that threatened to tear their shelter from its foundation and blow them clean to the Nueces.

Mary grew hysterical and began to scream. Then he started praying. Next, she cursed the wind, Texas, Brad, and God.

"I'm leaving when this is over," she said. "I hate

*Texas. I hate you for bringing me here. God, we're go-
ing to die, I know it."*

"We're not going to die, Mary."

"Damn you, Brad. You bastard. You had no business
bringing me out here to this desolate, godforsaken place.
Nobody can live here. My seeds have all blown away,
every last one of them."

She began to sob and he couldn't stand to see her
like that, but she beat at him with her fists when he tried
to comfort her and she cursed him until the sand-filled
air was blue.

Mary finally buried her face in her hands, doubled
over on the divan, and just kept crying. The wind blew
all afternoon and into the night and she finally fell
asleep, choking and gasping on the dust inside the
house. He covered her with a blanket when the rain and
hail began to pelt the house, rattling it from baseboard
to rafters.

The rain and the hail sounded like flung buckshot, and
the wind kept up, roaring in his ears as he wondered all
night if they were going to be struck by a twister. He
expected the house to be flattened at any minute, either
crushing them to death or leaving them at the mercy of
the wind. He imagined being sucked up into a dark fun-
nel and flung like dolls to the ground several miles away.
He had seen twisters do that to people and structures.

Sometime before dawn, the wind eased and the hail
melted on the ground as the rain shrank to a drizzling
patter. Mary awoke at dawn, when it grew suddenly
quiet as the storm passed on. She stood up, her hair in
tangles, and walked to the front window. She jerked the
blanket down. Dust danced in the air as it fell to the
floor. She looked out the window and saw bare paths
carved by the rushing water. Her garden was gone, the
dirt and seeds washed away. All that was left was a sheet
of glistening clay that had been beneath the topsoil. It
looked as if a flash flood had roared through, leaving
nothing behind but devastation.

"This place," she said, turning from the window. *"It's not fit for man or beast."*

Her words had sent a shudder through him that he could still feel, even at this moment.

A few moments later the front door opened and Brad felt the rush of air, the sting of the blown dust. Lou entered first, carrying Brad's rifle, saddlebags, and bedroll, followed by Paco and Gid, carrying their gear, stumbling into the room, propelled by wind and weariness. Lou shut the door and dropped Brad's things on the floor before rehanging a blanket over the door and scooting a soggy dirty towel against the bottom to keep the grit out.

"Thanks, Lou."

"Nice new rifle, Major."

"No more 'Major,' Lou. The war's over."

"I've got whiskey. I can make coffee. Gid, you're a sight for sore eyes. Last time I saw you, you were chasin' Yankees across the Rio."

"Did you meet Paco, Lou?"

Reeves looked at the Mexican and shook his head. He didn't offer his hand, and turned away. Brad didn't push it. Some Texians still did not like Mexicans or Spaniards or the French. It was an awkward moment and he felt sorry for Paco, but sometimes feelings got hurt when strangers first met up. He expected he might be able to change Lou's mind about Paco, at least, even if he couldn't remove the resentments he bore against all foreigners.

"What'll it be, Maj—Brad? Gid?"

"Whiskey's fine," Brad said.

"It's corn," Lou said.

"Fair enough."

"Anything wet's fine with me," Gid said.

"I'll put water in it," Lou called from the kitchen. "If Chambers didn't swaller it all."

"You've got enough water in there to float a small

boat," Brad said. Then, to Paco, *"Qué quieres, mi amigo? Agua? Café? Algo más fuerte?"*

"Nada," Paco replied. *"No quiero nada."*

"Don't you be jabberin' that Mex shit, Chambers," Lou said. "We speak American in my house."

Brad walked into the kitchen, retrieved a glass from a cupboard, and picked up the pitcher he had drunk from. He poured the glass full and set the pitcher down. "Paco's just as thirsty as Gid and me," he said. "You don't mind me showing him a little human kindness, do you, Lou?"

"I don't cotton to Mexes."

"He won't hurt you."

"Damned right." Lou finished pouring whiskey into three glasses and then he splashed some water in two of them. "Give that greaser all the goddamned water he wants, for all I care."

"Your compassion overwhelms me, Lou."

"Huh?"

"Skip it."

Brad walked into the front room and handed the glass of water to Paco. Paco nodded in gratitude and drank the whole glass in one swallow. "Want more?" Brad asked.

Paco shook his head, wiped his mouth, and handed the glass back to Brad. Brad set it down on a table and waited for Lou to hand him a glass of whiskey and water.

"Thanks, Lou," Brad said, taking the glass.

"You see all them papers on that table yonder?" Lou asked, handing a drink to Gid, keeping the straight one for himself.

Brad glanced at the table between the front room and the kitchen. "Yeah," he said, glancing at scattered sheafs of papers in disarray atop the table.

"Me'n Randy both got served them yesterday by a pack of Yankee carpetbaggers."

"What do the papers say?" Gid asked, sipping from

his drink. His eyes were rimmed with dust and dirt, giving him the appearance of a curious raccoon.

"They say we're going to lose our spreads for back taxes, all kinds of war assessments, you name it. Seems like the government, what still owes me soldier's pay, wants to grab my land. One of those jaspers had the goddamned gall to ask me if I would sell for a nickel an acre. When I told him no, he offered me a dime. I should have shot every one of the bastards, especially that goddamned traitor what was with 'em."

"You mean they can just take your land like that?" Gid asked.

Brad said nothing. He sat there, mulling over what Lou had said. He swallowed some of his branch and whiskey, then walked to the table and riffled through the papers.

"That's what they said," Lou replied. "Gave me ninety days to come up with the taxes I owe and all the other fees and assessments or they'll take my land for nothin'."

"Jesus," Gid said, as Brad picked up a document and read it.

Lou glanced over at Brad. "Well, don't that fair beat all, Brad?"

"It all looks official," Brad said. "And mighty suspicious."

"What do you mean?" Lou asked.

"Looks to me like someone's out to grab your land and pulled some strings in Austin."

"Anything I can do about it?"

"You can come work for me and pay up your liens and taxes."

"You got a job for me?"

"A manhunter's job," Brad said.

"Well, if it pays well enough, I'll surely do it. I didn't have much left when I got back. Randy neither."

"I know," Brad said. "Who was the traitor you mentioned? I thought you said these men were Yankees. Carpetbaggers."

"Well, the one what offered me a nickel and a dime an acre was a damned bluebelly, that's for sure. The other'n, he was like a-showin' this Yankee around. From the sound of his voice, I'd say he was a Texian."

"Did either of the men have names?"

"The Yankee carpetbagger was a man named Grimsby or something like that."

"What about the other one? The Texian?"

"I heard this Grimsby feller call him Thorne."

"Abel Thorne?" Brad asked.

"I didn't get no first name. Just Thorne."

Gid and Brad exchanged glances. Brad's mouth warped into a slow sidelong smile.

"What?" Lou asked.

"Abel Thorne, Lou. That's the man I'm after."

Lou sat down, stunned. Gid heaved a sigh and finished his drink. Paco walked over to a corner of the room and sat down. Brad stood there, listening to the howl of the wind.

Now, he thought, some things were starting to make sense. It would take some sorting out, but when the blow was over, they could ride to Randy Dunn's place and talk to him. If he came with them, they had a good chance of catching Thorne before he did any more damage.

But the whole thing was beginning to smell of politics and he didn't like it one damned bit.

12

RANDY DUNN LOOKED UP FROM THE ANVIL, TO SEE the riders emerge on the horizon, tiny moving specks at the edge of the flat plain that was now almost all mud from the rains of the night before. He twisted the tongs holding the horseshoe, bent it over the anvil, and hammered at the part of the shoe that was glowing cherry-red.

Sand and dust covered everything in sight. The winds had dropped off just before dawn, but they had kept him awake most of the night. He had put the horses up in the barn when the winds first started building and they had nickered and whinnied to get out in the corral while it was still dark. He knew that they must have had a miserable night, too. Underneath the wind, he could hear them trying to kick their stalls down to escape the dark confines of the barn. He still hadn't inspected everything, but at least the roofs of the house and barn hadn't blown away during the long night of ferocious winds.

Quickly, he dipped the hot shoe into the vat of cold, murky black water and listened to the metal hiss and sizzle. Then, he set the tongs down and checked his side-arm, a New Model Remington .44 that had been converted from percussion to centerfire.

Then he stepped inside the barn a few paces and reached for the heavy Henry rifle. He picked it up, jacked a cartridge into the chamber, and stepped further back into the shadows.

Dunn was a burly man, muscular, with a florid, round face, a small handlebar mustache, reddish hair that was almost the color of rusted iron, trimmed sideburns that turned to wire if he didn't keep them cropped down, pale blue eyes and a jutting chin that bore a crease at the bottom center.

"Now who in the hell can that be?" he said to himself, and checked his pistol again to see if it was loose in his holster. He looked at the specks on the horizon as they grew larger. But there was still no definition yet. He didn't know if there were three riders or four and he had to look away when he felt the strain on his eyes.

His boots were covered with mud, just like the rest of the yard around his house and barn. He had been up on the roof before dawn repairing a leak that started during the night when the rain poured through a hole left by a shingle that had been ripped away by the wind and hail.

The riders were coming from the direction of Lou's place, but that didn't mean anything. He didn't expect Lou to come by today. They had talked out their visits by that Yankee carpetbagger, the traitorous Thorne, and his *pistolero* compadres. He had flat-out told Thorne that if he wanted his land, he'd have to come and take it by force and he would shoot the first son-of-a-bitch that came again with papers, be it a marshal or a land grabber.

But, if this was more trouble from that bunch, they sure as hell weren't waiting no ninety days to foreclose on him, the bastards. He had bought this land with hard-earned cash and had paid for it many times over in blood and sweat. By the gods, no Yankee carpetbagger was going to take it away from him, not as long as he was alive, anyway. He had defended against Apaches and Comanches before the war and he wasn't going to give it up because of a few pieces of paper. The land was all he had, all he cared about, and he would die before he would just give it away. He had fought in a war to keep it out of Yankee hands and he'd fight for it again until he drew his last breath.

The horses warned him.

He had a half-dozen Mexican horses in the corral and they started kicking up a ruckus that woke him up before dawn. The mares were screaming, the colts were bleating in high-pitched squeals, and the gelding was whinnying in his gruff voice that signified danger. One of the mares was trying to kick the poles down. When he looked out, he saw the horses milling and smashing their bodies against the gate.

His first thought was that a rattlesnake had come into the corral; then he thought of wolves. It was just beginning to get light, but he was already dressed, had eaten breakfast, and was having a last taste of coffee. He strapped on his cap and ball .36 caliber Navy Colt and grabbed the double-barreled Greener by the door. It was loaded with double-ought buckshot and he knew the powder was dry because he had just loaded it the night before. Snakes had been a problem all that spring, with copperheads and pygmy rattlers coming out of the low wetlands to get at his chickens in the henhouse, or to catch the rats and mice that had taken shelter under the house during the winter.

He spoke to the horses as he approached and one or two of them settled down. He stepped inside the corral, climbing through the poles.

"What's the matter?" he said, his voice soft and soothing. "Did you see a snake?"

The horses seemed reassured by his presence and he spoke to each one, patting them on their necks, and that's when he saw them, two at first, then two more, out of the corner of his eye. Apaches on foot, skulking toward the corral.

He stood next to one of the horses, his hand on its withers. The horse was between him and the approaching Indians. He reasoned that if he stood still, he could not be seen easily in the dim light of the dawn.

Two Apaches rose up and, bent over, ran a few yards, then dropped out of sight. Then, the next two, farther back, did the same thing. He waited, wishing now he had grabbed up his rifle instead of the Greener.

But then he realized he'd have only one shot with the Kentucky flintlock. At least with the scattergun, he'd have two shots. And he still had the six-gun.

The Apaches kept coming, using that same pattern. So now he knew how many and how they planned to steal his horses. Two of the horses whinnied and looked toward the Indians. As soon as they did, the Apaches dropped down out of sight again.

The other horses began to mill around, but the one he was gentling with his hand stayed put, content to remain under his protection. As long as the others were moving, he thought, the Apaches would be watching them and might fail to notice him standing next to one of them, out of their line of sight.

It began to get lighter by the moment. The Apaches were perhaps still a good two hundred yards away. By pairs, they rose up and ran a few yards, then lay on the ground, out of sight. Two, then the other two. The horses began to fidget again as the Apaches came closer, but the gelding still held its position, although now it was stamping one foot on the ground, then pawing the dirt with its right hoof.

As the land began to brighten, Randy saw movement on the horizon beyond the skulking Apaches. As the morning gradually began to lighten, his heart sank. The Apaches had not walked here, but had ridden, and there was at least one of their band holding the horses for those now afoot. They were specks on the horizon at that distance, but the silhouettes were clearly those of horses and one man, perhaps two, held them in readiness. He saw only one man, but admitted to himself that there could be two. And, he asked himself silently, how many more were waiting out of sight, beyond the dip of the land?

The Apaches were patient; he'd give them that. Agonizing moments crawled by as he waited for the red men to get within range of his scattergun. His palms began to sweat and the Greener turned lead-heavy. His knees jellied as his legs started to quiver. He had stood stock-still so long, he wanted to run, to bring back the feeling to his legs, to somehow set the cold blood in his veins to flowing again.

The Apaches crawled still closer. He could catch only slices of movement, since he dared not move his head. Then they came so close he could hear them, or else he imagined he heard them. A rustle of grass, a scrape of a moccasin, the rub of a bare arm on the earth.

The horses stopped pacing and turned to face the skulking Apaches, their ears twisting to pick up each small sound. Then the agitated horses ran at him and the horse next to him moved out of the way. Suddenly he was in the open, exposed, and he dropped to one knee as the grass exploded with four Apaches leaping to their feet, arrows nocked, bows drawn.

The Indians screeched high-pitched yelps as they charged the corral. They shot their arrows at him on the run. He took a bead on the nearest man, cocked both barrels of the Greener, and fired the first one. The gun bucked in his hands, spewing out white smoke and deadly shot. The buckshot nearly tore the charging Apache apart at less than ten yards, cutting off his yips and scattering blood, bone, flesh, and guts in a wide arc, like flung entrails. He swung the barrel on the second man and touched the trigger. The Apache threw up both hands as the lead ripped into his face and throat, tearing them apart in a cloud-spray of rosy blood.

He stood up then and drew his pistol, cocking it as it cleared the holster. He led the next man and squeezed off a shot. Without waiting to see if he had struck his target, he turned to the last of the four Apaches, who was charging toward him with a long skinning knife poised to strike. The Apache's blood-curdling scream stopped with the explosion of the pistol. The ball caught him square in the Adam's apple and he stopped, spun around, flailing at the sky, the knife still clutched in his hand, gasping for breath and drawing in only blood that made a whistling sound in his throat.

He turned to the third man and saw him down on the ground, still alive, crawling painfully toward him. He rushed up to him, put the barrel of the pistol to the man's temple, and squeezed off the shot. The Apache's head burst open like a melon struck with a ten-pound maul, spraying blood and gray matter for two yards as the other side of his head blew away like a pie plate.

Something moving caught the corner of his eye. He looked up and saw the Apache horses start to run. The Apache who had been watching them yelled something, then disappeared from sight. He heard the sound of pounding hoofbeats, then two rifle shots that sounded like firecrackers. Two more Apaches appeared on the horizon, running at high speed. Then he saw them both stumble and fall. A split second later he heard two rifle reports, very close together.

As he stood there, watching, two riders appeared. They stopped by the fallen Apaches, then started riding toward him. He cocked his pistol and waited.

"You there," called one of the riders. "Are you all right?"

"Yeah."

He waited until the riders got close enough for him to see that they were white men. They rode up on him and he saw two men, one young, the other a little older, their faces covered with three-day beards and dust, their rifles still smoking.

"You are one lucky son-of-a-bitch," the older man said, looking at the dead Apaches outside the corral. *"And a damned good shot, 'pears to me."*

"Who in hell are you?"

"I'm Ford. He's Chambers. We've been tracking these red niggers for twenty mile."

"Why?"

"We're Texas Rangers," Chambers said. *"These Apaches killed a family over by San Antone."*

"How many did you kill over yonder?"

"Four," Chambers said. *"They were getting ready to ride down here and slit your gullet."*

"They needed fresh horses," Ford said. *"Looks like they picked your string, fella. Glad they didn't add your scalp to their belts. You got any coffee with maybe some whiskey to sweeten it up? We haven't slept in two days. Onliest thing holding us up is our belts and these tired old horses."*

Funny that he would think of that first meeting with Ford and Brad Chambers. But the riders coming toward him reminded him of that day.

One of the men started waving as they came closer and he recognized Lou Reeves. He waved back.

Moments later, he saw Brad Chambers lift a hand in greeting. Then he saw Gid. He didn't know the Mexican.

"Well, well, look what the wind done blown in," Randy said. "Is this meetin' day? Did you boys have an appointment?"

"Randy, you haven't changed a bit," Brad said. "I see the wind didn't blow you away last night."

"Light down," Randy said. "What brings you to these parts, Major?"

Brad didn't swing out of the saddle right away. Instead, he looked Randy straight in the eye and said: "Abel Thorne. Wondered if you might want to join us on a manhunt. Full army pay."

"Rebel or Yankee?" Randy asked.

"Does it make any difference?"

"Not a damned bit. As long as I don't have to wear no uniform, Major."

"It's a come-as-you-was party, Randy."

"You aim to catch this Abel Thorne?"

"Dead or alive," Brad said, and swung down out of the saddle. He was not smiling.

13

Abel Thorne jerked the reins, bringing his horse to a sudden halt at the edge of a large clearing. Beyond the tree stumps, near the opposite edge, stood a small clapboard house that appeared to have been made with scrap lumber. It had a sod roof and an uneven porch with three handmade chairs.

A mongrel dog lay under the porch, eyeing the men who had ridden up. It did not bark or wag its tail. Beyond the house, there were no stumps, but a three- or four-acre cleared spot. Two Negroes were working the garden, hoeing and raking along the rows of corn, beans, okra, cabbage, and other vegetables. They looked up and stood unmoving.

Thorne turned to the man in the suit who had ridden up alongside him.

"This isn't on my list," the man said.

"Grimley, you can stay or ride around and we'll meet up with you. But me and the boys have business here."

"What business would that be, Mr. Thorne?"

"My business. If you don't want to watch, then you'd better ride on around. You know where the road is."

Jonas Grimley, a pudgy-lipped man of florid com-

plexion, with sagging jowls and a crisply trimmed
square mustache, flat sideburns and a pair of tiered chins,
pulled a handkerchief from his coat pocket and dabbed
at the beads of sweat glistening in the wrinkled furrows
of his forehead. He cleared his throat of accumulated
phlegm and adjusted his portly body in the cradle of the
Denver saddle.

"Well, I don't know, Mr. Thorne. I do not wish to
ride alone in such wild and unfamiliar country. Do you
know these people?"

"I know them as nigger squatters, Grimley. Now make
up your mind. You can stay and be a part of this or ride
on and never know the difference."

"You mean you don't want me to witness a crime."

"I mean that."

"Mr. Thorne, as a duly sworn and designated official
of the United States government, I strongly . . ."

"I don't want to hear that shit, Grimley. Now, either
get your ass back to the road and ride around these nigger squatters, or you join us and bear the blame."

"I will not be a party to any . . ."

"I ain't goin' to tell you again, Grimley. You ought
to catch up with Blackjack and the pack horse. He
should be waitin' at the next crossroads. You wait there.
We'll be along directly."

"I have another farm on my list that ought to be
nearby. The Worth place, I believe."

"Worth's is the next farm over, but we have to go to
the crossroads to reach it. You let me worry about where
we go next, Grimley. Now, get on. Tell Blackjack we'll
be along directly."

Grimley spluttered, but said nothing. He took one
more look at the two Negroes standing in their garden
and turned his horse to ride the connecting path back to
the road.

Thorne watched him go, then beckoned to his two
companions. They rode up alongside. One of them, a
man named Herbert Luskin, wore a smirk on his pock-

marked face. The other, Orville Trask, bore a full-toothed grin that, with his off-center left eye, gave his face a lopsided appearance. His face appeared to have been mashed together out of spare parts, a deformity granted him at birth when a drunken barber, in his capacity as a surgeon, squeezed his head while pulling him out of his mother's womb.

"Boy oh boy," Trask said, "you done found us some bluegums, Abel."

"Shut your mouth, Orv," Thorne said. "Wait'll that damned Yankee gets on down the road a ways."

Thorne shot Trask a withering scowl, and when Luskin opened his mouth to say something, Thorne pierced him with a lancing look that made the darkness of midnight look like daylight. "You neither, Herb."

Thorne was a lean whip of a man who looked as if he had been cut from a mean bolt of cloth with a hatchet slice. He was all angles, from his bony arms and pole-thin legs to his high cheekbones framing a square jaw that was bent inward in the shape of a wedge. His small dark eyes were deep-sunk, seemingly radiating the meanness of his black soul. Despite his slender build, he was intimidating in the sinister way that a venomous snake can strike fear in its prey.

The three men listened to the sound of the receding hoofbeats. When it was silent, Thorne turned to look at the two farmers in their garden. He lifted a hand and waved. Trask suppressed a chuckle. After a moment, the man in the garden raised his hand and waved back. Thorne dug his spurs into his horse's flanks and rode toward the couple. He, like the other two men, carried two rifles in scabbards attached to both sides of his saddle. Each man wore two pistols on belts, and each had sidearms dangling from his saddlehorn in holsters.

"Do I get to shoot one?" Luskin asked.

"If you want," Thorne said. "I'll open the ball. You boys just wait."

"You aimin' to have some sport with 'em first, Abel?" Trask asked.

"I aim to give 'em what for," Thorne said, as a sudden thought crossed his mind.

The auctioneer walked around the naked black man as light streamed through the chinks in the old barn's roof and walls, shooting spears of light on the men who stood there in a cluster watching the proceedings.

"Here we have a young buck, around eighteen years of age, in his prime, with strong legs and back, in good health, with good teeth and big hands. He'll pick your cotton, build your fences, dig your wells, slop your hogs, chop wood, service your young slave gals, and live to a ripe old age."

The auctioneer grabbed the youth's scrotum and hefted it in his hand as if it were a chunk of meat.

"What am I bid, what'll it be, better get it, two, I hear two doodle a quarter now a half, biddle de bid, will he do it, three, ba ba bid it three and do I hear it?" Talking very fast, just a stream of talk with numbers in it.

"Daddy, why do people buy other people?"

"Abel, these ain't people," his father said. "They're Negroes, wild critters come over on a boat from Africa, same as cattle."

"But they look like people, only they got black skin."

"Son, don't you never forget, these niggers ain't human. They was born to be slaves to white folks and that's why we buy and sell 'em. God put 'em here on this earth to work for white folk."

"Daddy, would you sell me?"

"Abel, Abel, how come you to talk that way? You ain't no nigger. I'd never sell you. Nobody would buy you, anyways."

"How come?"

"Why, you ain't nothing but a little bitty old thing and you're white as white can be. White people ain't slaves. Only niggers."

"Yes, sir."

"Sold," said the auctioneer. *"One thousand dollars."*

"Don't you reach for no rifle or pistol until I tell you," Thorne said. "I don't want to have to chase down these niggers."

"No sir," Trask said. Luskin grunted his assent.

"Howdy," Thorne said as he rode up to the edge of the garden.

"Yes, suh, howdy," the black man said.

"You sharecroppin' here?"

"No, suh, we is free. We owns this land."

"No, by God, you don't," Thorne said, pulling the pistol from his right holster, easing it out slow.

"Suh?"

"You don't get no forty acres and a mule, you black son-of-a-bitch," Thorne said. "No matter what General Sherman said."

"Now?" Luskin asked.

"Now," Thorne said, cocking his pistol. He aimed at the black man and squeezed the trigger. The woman started to run toward her husband, but both Luskin and Trask opened up with their rifles and cut her down. She fell across her husband's body, her blood streaming from her neck and chest onto his legs.

"Make sure," Thorne said to Trask. Then he turned his horse without another glance and blew the smoke out of his barrel. He holstered his pistol and rode off. Behind him, Trask and Luskin shot two more times, striking the already dead couple in their heads.

The two caught up to Thorne and they rode the path down to the road.

"What was that about forty acres and a mule?" Luskin asked.

"That goddamned Sherman done went and guaranteed every goddamned nigger slave free land, the son-of-a-bitch. Well, by God, not in Texas. Not while I'm alive."

"No sir," Trask said.

"For Christ's sakes," Luskin said. "For Jesus Christ's sakes."

After they were gone, a white woman walked out of the woods, about a half hour later. She was leading a mule wearing a halter and rope behind her.

"Jessy?" she called. "Joe Sam?"

Puzzled, she led the mule toward the house, following a path on the far end of the garden. She saw something out of the corner of her eye and stopped.

"Jessy? Joe Sam?"

She dropped the rope and ran up one row of sprouted corn. She stopped when she saw the dead couple lying there. She saw the bullet holes in their heads, their vacant eyes, glassed over, glinting dully in the sun.

Then she dropped to her knees, buried her head in her hands, and began to weep.

14

BRAD HELPED RANDY PACK GRUB IN HIS SADDLEBAGS.

"I'm right glad you decided to join up with us, Randy," Brad said.

"I figgered something was wrong when that puffbag Grimley served those papers on me. Wasn't him, so much, but those three hardcases he had bracing him looked like trouble."

"Just four men, then?"

"Well, I seen another way off, a-leading a pack horse. He was with 'em, but he didn't ride up; he went on down the road toward Norm Worth's place. But, hell, that's a good fifty mile from here."

Brad swore.

"What?" Randy asked, as he tucked a flour sack full of hardtack into one of his saddlebags.

"Norm Worth's got a temper. He might not take kindly to Grimley serving him papers."

"No, I reckon not. Neither did I, but those three hard-cases looked ready to throw down on me if I blinked. 'Specially that one they called Abel."

Paco had wandered off to take a leak and Brad saw him walking back from behind Randy's barn. Lou and

Gid were still talking about the windstorm while their horses nibbled on grain from Randy's stable.

"Get on your horse, Paco," Brad said. "Gid, you and Lou about ready?"

"We're ready," Gid said.

Brad turned back to Randy. "We may be gone a while, Randy. Thorne and his bunch have got a good head start on us."

"I figger they had to hole up yesterday and last night."

"Where might that be?"

"Well, 'tween here and the Worth spread, there are some old adobes we used to use as line shacks during roundup and when we cut brush. Then, there's Jessy and Joe Sam Cooper's place. But they wouldn't hole up there, even if they could have made it that far."

"How come?"

Randy's face took on a quizzical look. "Cooper don't owe no back taxes. He's a freed slave livin' on land the government give him. Got him a shack and a garden, a mule and a plow."

"Christ, Randy."

"You think Thorne and Grimley might go there?"

"Abel Thorne's pa was a damned slave trader. Thorne's got no use for the Negro race, to hear him tell it."

"That don't sound good, Major."

"Let's see if we can pick up Thorne's tracks by and by," Brad said. He walked to his horse and pulled himself up into the saddle.

In moments, the five men were heading to the southwest, over ground blown trackless by the winds of the day and night before.

They followed an old wagon road that was still used by some, for it cut through groves of mesquite sprung up from seeds dropped by longhorn cattle in their dung as they wandered the open spaces seeking grass long before Americans began settling in Texas. But the ruts were long gone, the road worn down by riders traveling between the scattered ranches and farms that the valley now harbored in the wake of long dead pioneers who had left their bones and their blood on the plain, along with Apaches and Comanches, horses and cattle whose skulls lay bleached white and scattered like broken pottery from the Rio Grande to the Nueces River and beyond.

Brad began looking for tracks, but only saw those of the roadrunner, the jackrabbit, the coyote, and the wild turkey. Ten miles further on, they passed an old adobe, its sod roof caved in, its bricks crumbling to dust, and still no horse tracks, nor any sign that men had passed that way.

"There's another adobe, in better shape, about two mile ahead," Randy said. "Might be a hidey place."

"I'm counting on it," Brad said, his voice flat; the expression on his face seemed to be coated with a patina of grimness, as if shadowed by a passing cloud.

After another hour, Brad called a halt and told his companions to have a smoke. He rolled a quirly for himself as he surveyed the land ahead and mentally calculated how far they had come.

"This isn't strictly a military operation," he said, "but I think I'd better issue some orders."

"Orders?" Gid asked.

Brad's lips curled in a faint smile. "Suggestions."

Randy and Lou laughed right away. Gid looked at them and then laughed himself. Paco's expression did not change, rigid as ever.

"Gid, you ride drag. I'll ride point with Randy, who knows the country better than any of us. Lou, you take the right flank, but keep within twenty yards or so. Paco, you ride on my left. I think we need some eyes looking around us from now on. Agreed?"

"Sounds like a good order to me," Lou said, grinning.

"Probably a damned good idea," Randy said. "This damned Texas brush can hide a whole lot of things."

"I don't mind riding in the rear," Gid said, "as long as it don't last forever."

Brad looked at him. "You don't like riding drag?"

"I don't like looking at horses' asses all damned day."

Brad and the others laughed, including Paco, this time.

"Which horses' asses are you talking about?" Brad asked.

"Well, not you, Major," Gid said, looking at the others. And they all laughed again.

"That's good to know," Brad said. "Although I'm a pretty good horse's ass at times."

"Most of the time," Randy said, and there was more laughter as the men smoked and their horses switched their tails at the biting flies, their muscles quivering to shake off those that their tails could not reach.

The men finished their smokes and when Brad gave the signal, they dropped into formation. Randy looked at Gid in the rear and at Lou and Paco on their flanks. "Looks like a military expedition to me," he said.

"It may well turn out that way, Randy," Brad said.

"I can't get over you and Phil Sheridan. Times sure do change."

"And the man who doesn't change with them gets left behind," Brad said.

"I ain't never goin' to be no Yankee."

"Neither am I, Randy. I think the idea is to be an American. The war's over and we've got to set aside our differences with the North and get on with our lives."

"First, though, we have to take care of these damned carpetbaggers."

"No, first we take care of Abel Thorne," Brad said firmly.

"Yeah, I reckon."

"How much farther to that other adobe?" Brad asked.

"Another mile or two, maybe. I haven't been this way in a while and that windstorm did some rearranging of real estate. Like that live oak over there. It seems a mite more bent over than I recollect."

Brad laughed. "Yeah," he said, "things change. Even the land."

A half hour later, Randy put out his arm to stop Brad. Brad held up his hand and the others reined in their horses. It was very quiet and Randy did not speak for several seconds.

"There's that adobe, yonder," Randy said, "just beyond that clump of low mesquite. You look close, you can just see a corner of it."

"I see it," Brad said, his voice barely above a whisper.

"Don't look to be nobody there," Randy said.

"Could be a nest of rattlesnakes inside," Brad said. "You wouldn't see or hear them until it was too late."

"I see what you mean. What do you want to do then?"

"Let's take it slow and easy. You and Lou go around those trees and come up on the right side. If you see any tracks, stay off them. I'll send Paco and Gid around the left to flank me."

"You going to ride straight on in?"

"Yeah. It's one way to find out if anybody's inside. If I draw fire, you come at a lick."

Randy nodded.

Brad turned to Gid and motioned to him. Gid rode up. Brad told him what he wanted him and Paco to do. Lou rode over then. "You and Randy circle those trees and come up on the right of that little adobe yonder," Brad said.

"I don't see no adobe," Lou said.

"Trust me, Lou. It's there. Easy does it. I'll ride up slow and we'll see what's what."

Brad watched the others ride away on either side of him. When he was satisfied they were far enough on their courses, he clucked to his horse and moved forward up the road. He loosened the Colt in its holster and kept his hand alongside in case he had to draw it quick.

As he rode closer, more of the abandoned adobe shack came into view. He angled left, so that he could see more of it. So far, so good, he thought, but he could hear his own breathing and the heartbeat in his left temple. He was traveling at such a slow pace that his horse's hooves made very little sound. If anyone was asleep inside, they might not hear him come up. If he was careful.

Gradually, he gained a three-quarters view of the adobe. Its roof was thick with sod and had not caved in, so it offered shelter from the rain or hail. Its bricks were worn from wind and weather; the windows were boarded up, so that he could not see inside either the side window or the one in back. He studied the ground and saw no tracks other than old, deep ones that were now filled with soil but still had some definition. Some were cart tracks, others were cattle and horse tracks made during some long-ago time when mud covered the road thick enough so that the impressions held, baked hard by the sun after the rains that made the mud.

As he drew ever closer to the adobe hut, Brad closed his hand around the butt of his pistol. His breathing grew shallow and his gut tightened until it was rock-hard. He watched his horse's ears as they twisted, turning to pick up any sound. He no longer saw his companions and he felt very alone as he rode the last few yards to the house. He turned his head slightly and then twisted quickly in the saddle. There was that shadow again, or so he thought, off to his right. But when he looked he saw nothing, no one. Still, he had the strong sense that someone was watching him and he could not shake the feeling. His eyes told him he was mistaken, but his mind clouded over with the thought that he was being watched.

As he rode close to the adobe, his horse grew skittery and balked, stepping sideways in a wary sidle. Brad sniffed the air as a barrage of scents assailed his nostrils. He fought the horse back to his original course, reining him hard to turn him; when the animal calmed down,

Brad knew what he was smelling: human excrement, fresh and odorous.

He rode around to the front of the adobe and drew his pistol. The front door was missing and, with the sun on the other side, the interior was dark, seemingly vacant. He saw no horses, but when he looked down at the ground around the adobe, he saw many tracks and piles of horse dung and bare places where they had urinated.

He looked up and saw Lou and Randy just coming into view. He holstered his pistol and waved them on in. Then he turned and saw Paco and Gid off to the left. He beckoned for them to ride up. He dismounted and let his reins trail as he started to walk toward the doorway of the adobe.

The smell of urine was strong inside the adobe. Slivers of light shone through the boarded-up windows. When his eyes became adjusted to the darkness, he saw where the men had laid out their bedrolls. He saw and smelled food and there was the scent of smoke. They had built a fire in the fireplace, a small one from the looks of the ashes, and scattered around were empty airtights that had once contained peaches and prunes. The stench inside was strong. Mingled with the scents of urine and food, was the pungent aroma of candle wax.

Now, he thought, *what would they need candlelight for, if they had a fire going?* He walked around, looking for anything that might not have been there before the men stopped to get out of the wind. Something caught his eye and he walked over to a place near the hearth and picked up a scrap of paper. He couldn't read it in the poor light.

Brad stepped back outside. "They stayed here last night."

"Yeah, I can see their tracks," Randy said. "They're all over."

Brad studied the tracks for several moments. Then he looked up at the men sitting their horses.

"They have a pack horse that's carrying a lighter load

this morning. So they have plenty of food. They can go a long way, I figure."

"How far ahead of us do you think they are?" Gid asked.

"Maybe three hours," Brad said.

"This place sure stinks," Lou said.

"What you got in your hand?" Randy asked. "A piece of paper, looks like."

Brad held the piece of paper up so that he could study it. "It's a map," he said. "Or part of one. Take a look, Randy."

Brad walked over to Randy's horse and handed Randy the scrap of paper. Randy looked at it, turned it upside down and sideways.

"Well?" Brad asked.

"Jesus," Randy said. "Here's the road we come up, and there's the Worth place, and next to it, on this side, a little path leading to where the Coopers live."

"Are you sure?" Brad asked.

"Did you look at it real close?" Randy asked. "Them little squares have writin' under 'em."

"I didn't notice," Brad said. "What's the writing say?"

Randy handed the fragment of paper back to Brad. "Under the big square's a W. That stands for Worth and is right on the road. That little square has a C on it. For Cooper. And what looks like bushes or something, is the word 'niggers.' "

Brad held the scrap close to his face. There was a line drawn from the road straight to the square labeled "C."

"Makes your blood run cold, don't it?" Randy asked.

"Like ice," Brad replied.

15

NORM WORTH HAD THREE STUMPS ON FIRE AND ALL three were smoking. He had poured coal oil on them the day before, then the wind had come up, so he didn't light them until that morning. In the windless air, the columns of gray-blue smoke rose straight to the sky. It would take a good three days to burn the stumps out of the ground, but he had dug around them so that the fire could get plenty of air.

He had borrowed Cooper's mule to pull some of the small stumps, but these were the big ones, live oaks that he'd had to clear. He and Cal, his son, had sawed them off clear to the ground, but they were a nuisance and had to be removed.

And where in hell was Cal, anyway? That kid was scarce as hen's teeth when there was work to be done. And Hollie was taking her sweet time getting that sorry mule back to Joe Cooper's place. Hell, it wasn't more'n two mile through the woods.

"Cal?" Norm called.

There was no answer.

"Calvin? Where in hell are you, boy? Are you playin' with your pud again?"

"Hoooo," Cal called, from deep inside the barn, it sounded like.

"Fetch me some more coal oil," Norm yelled.

"Comin', Pa."

Cal Worth emerged from the barn carrying a glass jug half full of coal oil that had a cork in it. The oil sloshed as he ambled toward his father. Norm started digging in his overalls for a box of matches, but he kept his eyes on his gangly son, a boy of seventeen, motherless since he was fifteen.

Norm's wife, Abigail, had died of the pox in 1863. She had been a frail woman and had caught the disease, Norm thought, in Galveston when they all went there in the buggy to buy supplies for their farm. Hollie had been nineteen when her mother died, and she had taken her place, doing all the cooking and laundry, and tending to the garden.

Cal handed the jug to his father. Norm waved it away. "Go over yonder and pour about two cups full on that stump what ain't burnin' so good."

"Which one is that?"

"Hell, boy, can't you see? The one where the smoke ain't no more'n knee-high."

Of course Cal went to the wrong stump and his father had to berate him and direct him to the right one. Cal poured nearly half the jug on the stump, drowning out the weak fire. Norm stalked over to it and glared at Cal. "Put the cork back in that jug," he said.

"Yes, sir," Cal said. He was not as tall as his father, who stood at five foot ten, all muscle from hard work, with thick bushy eyebrows and a shock of brown hair that Hollie tried to keep cut, but which grew straight and long down to his shoulders. Norm was clean-shaven, with steel-blue eyes, thin lips, and a small chin that came to a sharp point. Cal resembled his mother, but his features were weak and he tended to put weight on his middle so that he had a slight paunch. Norm knew that Cal wasn't right in the head. He'd had a difficult birth and nearly died of suffocation when Abigail couldn't strain him out of her womb. Norm had hoped Cal would grow out of his slowness, but was resigned to the fact that his son would always be slightly addled and just a hair or two off plumb.

"Who's coming', Pa?" Cal asked.

"Don't know. Just be quiet."

Norm listened to the crunch of grit and gravel, the familiar *clop, clop* of iron-shod hooves. Then he saw the first horse appear carrying a heavyset man he did not know. Then, three more horses and three strangers, all well-armed.

"Do you see 'em, Pa?"

"It doesn't look good, Cal. Just stay back. We'll see what these jaspers have to say."

"Hello," called the first man. "Mr. Worth?"

"That's far enough. State your business," Norm said.

"Are you Norman Worth?" The horses all stopped.

"What if I am?"

"Then I have important business with you, Mr. Worth. My name's Jonas Grimley and I'm from the government."

"What government might that be, Mr. Grimley?"

"The United States Government, sir."

"It don't take no four men to deliver no government papers."

"Sir, these men are here to safeguard me."

"Well, you tell them to go on, and you ride up real slow and show me them papers. I ain't goin' to hurt you."

Grimley turned to one of the men and whispered something to him that Norm couldn't hear, then turned back to face him again.

"Sir, if you'll just step out and let me give you these papers, we'll be on our way," Grimley said to Worth.

"What are the papers about?"

"Taxes, sir. You owe taxes on your land and your place here."

"Cal, you listen up real good," Norm said to his son. "You sneak out the back of the barn and go in the back of the house and stay there."

"How come, Pa?"

"You just do as you're told. Now git."

Cal shook his head and ambled toward the rear of the barn. Norm reached for the shot-loaded rifle. His hand touched the barrel and he left it there.

"This won't take long," Grimley said.

"No, it ain't goin' to take long at all, Mr. Grimley. Because I ain't comin' out, and unless you send those hardcases back to the road, you ain't goin' to serve me no papers."

"Let's be reasonable, sir," Grimley said.

"That's as reasonable as I aim to be," Norm replied.

More whispering among the men on horseback.

"Tell you what," Grimley said. "You've got what? Four thousand acres here, more or less?"

"More or less," Norm said.

"I'll make you an offer. Cash on the barrelhead. I'll give you five cents an acre, throw in a hundred dollars for the house and barn. That's probably more than the lumber is worth. A fair price and you won't have any taxes to pay. You can take that money and start up someplace else, free and clear."

"Mr. Grimley," Norm said, "my place ain't for sale."

"If you don't pay the taxes on it, the government will take it anyway, and I can buy it for much less. I'd just pay the taxes on it."

"Did you come here to insult me?" Norm said. "Or are you just a goddamned thief?"

Grimley's face swelled and flushed a roseate hue. He turned to the men behind him and spoke a few words just above a whisper.

Norm's fingers closed around the barrel of the rifle. Then, as he was pulling the gun toward him, Grimley turned his horse and started to ride away. The other men stayed where they were.

"Where's he goin'?" Norm asked.

"He don't want to see no bloodshed here," Thorne said.

"Onliest blood's goin' to be shed here is your'n, if'n you don't turn right around and foller him out of here."

Norm eased the rifle next to his leg.

"Y'all get off my property," Norm said. "Right now."

He pulled the rifle up with his right hand and was just grabbing it with his left to bring it to his shoulder when the three men kicked their horses in the flanks and drew pistols.

Before Norm could touch the stock to his shoulder, all three men started shooting at him. He started to duck back into the barn, when a ball struck him in the left leg. He felt as if someone had driven a large nail into the bone. An intense pain suffused his leg and he felt paralyzed. He staggered as lead balls spanged the ground around him and ripped through the wood of the barn next to him.

Norm spun around, shifting his weight to his good right leg. When he looked up, through eyes blurred with pain, he saw the three men galloping toward him. He saw flashes of orange and puffs of white smoke spewing from their pistols and then a series of hammer blows struck his belly, arm, and shoulder. Then, as he began to fall, a ball struck him full in the chest and he felt the air rush out of his lungs. There was no more pain for a brief moment as he fell backward, unable to draw another breath.

From somewhere, just as a great darkness began to descend upon him, he thought he heard Cal calling out to him. Then he shivered in a final convulsion and fell into an eternity of blackness that erased all memory in a single instant.

16

THE TRACKS THAT MORNING AFTER THE WINDSTORM were easy to follow and Brad kept his men and the horses at a brisk pace. Besides, he now had a crude map in hand, and Randy knew the country. Even without the tracks, Brad knew where Thorne and his men were heading, and his stomach swirled with a queasy nervousness as he closed the distance. Thorne's tracks kept getting fresher and fresher, but Brad knew they were far behind and, unless Thorne stopped often, or dallied, they were not likely to catch up with him for a good four hours or so. From reading the signs, Brad knew that Thorne was eating up the miles at an even faster pace, even with the pack horse in tow.

The map, of course, did not give Brad any sense of the distance to either the Cooper or the Worth place, but Randy had told him they'd have a good ten miles to cover before they reached the Cooper farm. A good two hours' ride in the Texas heat, Brad knew.

As near as he could figure, Thorne and the others had left the abandoned adobe before dawn, when the dew was still sparkling on the earth. Now, the tracks had dried and they were crisp and sharp in the soft earth that was hardening by the minute.

A little past midmorning, the whole picture changed.

Brad reined up suddenly, catching Randy and the others by surprise. He turned his horse around and leaned over, studying the tracks. "Uh-oh," he said.

"What's wrong, Major?" Randy asked, as the others rode up.

"I almost missed it," Brad said, pointing to the ground. Then he rode back the way they had come, studying the ground until he came to another halt. "Here," he said. "The pack horse pulled out and headed south."

"So?" Randy asked.

"And where you are, another rider dismounted while the others rode on. I'll show you." Brad rode back up to where he'd been.

"I don't see anything," Randy said.

"One horse stopped here. A man got off and then lay flat next to the road. See the faint impression where he lay? And look here. He put his head down there."

All of the others looked, and then shook their heads.

"Thorne knows we're following him," Brad said.

"How do you know?" Gid asked.

"This one here put his ear to the ground. He could hear us. He waited until Thorne and two others rode far enough ahead. See, his tracks are fresher. He waited until it was quiet and then he listened. And he heard us."

"Then what?"

"Then, he lit a shuck to catch up to the other two."

"What about the pack horse?" Lou asked.

Brad sighed and tipped his hat back on his head, scratching at his temple. "I think Thorne had a hunch he was being followed and he sent the pack horse off to meet them somewhere south of where they're going. And he doesn't much care if we follow it. But he probably knows we won't. Then he or one of his men got down here to confirm his suspicions. I expect Thorne will step up the pace some now."

"Well, so can we," Lou said.

Brad looked up at the sun, shading his eyes. "Whatever Thorne had planned to do up at Cooper's or Worth's, he's already done," he said. "And nothing we can do about it."

"It's for sure, we can't catch up to him before he gets to Cooper's," Randy said. "So, now what?"

Brad shoved his hat back square. "Play it out, I reckon. See how fast he's traveling up ahead and then talk to Cooper and Worth and get an idea of when Thorne and his bunch showed up."

"You sound like a damned Ranger," Gid said.

"Well, this is Ranger work," Brad said. "Tracking, finding, apprehending."

"It's that 'apprehending' that old Thorne's goin' to buck," Gid said.

"Sometimes," Brad said, "you have to apprehend a culprit when he's no longer breathing."

"Huh?" Gid scratched his nose.

"He means dead, Gid," Lou said.

"I reckon that's how you're going to have to apprehend Thorne, then," Gid said. "He don't sound like the type who's just goin' to throw up his hands and say 'hang me.' "

"No, I reckon not," Brad said, and wheeled his horse back on to the road. "Let's go find out."

Wakefield pointed to a lone adobe on the outskirts of Del Rio. "Well, that's where he is, Brad. Holed up in that adobe yonder. Do you want to go in and get him?"

"What in hell are you talking about, Bob?"

"I mean the man we've been huntin', Leo Talley, has done run off the Mexicans what were livin' there and he's sittin' at a table by the winder with all his pistols laid out on the table and his rifle in his hands, the snout of it just below the windersill. All he's waitin' for is to

hear you call him out to surrender in the name of the law."

"I'll be damned if he is, Wakefield."

"Well, did you see that curtain move? He's there, all right. His tracks don't go no farther."

"And Talley's just going to walk out of there and give himself up?"

"If you ask him real polite, he might."

"You're full of the worst kind of shit, Bobby."

"Well, what are you goin' to do then? You're packin' a star. You're the law. And Talley's a damned criminal."

They were sitting their horses a good hundred and fifty yards from the adobe, which sat on a little hill above the river. It looked deserted. There were no signs of life, just a few chickens in a pen, and they were nestled in dust bowls like quail, sleeping. There was no dog, no cat, no milk cow. Just a few flowers in pots out front.

"How do you know his tracks stop there? And that Talley's inside?"

"I know he didn't swim the river. See that little flick of a tail back of the adobe?"

"No."

"Just keep lookin'."

"I see something moving. I don't know if it's a tail or not. A tail of what?"

"That's Talley's flea-bitten, slat-ribbed horse tied up back there switchin' at flies. He's probably got him hob-bled and snubbed."

"Could be, Bobby. The more I see it, the more it could be a horse's tail all right. But it might not be Talley's."

"I'll bet he's got him some Mexes tied up inside with socks stuffed in their mouths to keep 'em quiet."

"You're guessing."

"Well, maybe. But I've tracked men and bear who won't give up, even when they're cornered. This Talley, he's maybe killed five or six men or more, including at least one lawman over in Laredo, and he knows there's

*a rope waitin' in his regular collar size. He's not goin'
to give up."*

"So why do you want me to call him out?"

"I was just joshin' you, Brad. But there's your man
in there and I've got silver in my pocket that says he's
sittin' at that winder just waitin' for us to ride up on
him."

"He's wanted alive. To stand trial."

"Stubborn, ain't you, Brad? Well, if you want him
alive, you're goin' to have to ask him to surrender."

*The horse's rump backed away from the adobe. It was
Talley's horse all right. And that was its tail switching
at the flies razing its backside on a summer afternoon.*

"We can wait him out, Bob."

"Yeah, we can do that. It would mean one of us'd
have to go into town and bring grub out to the other.
Come nightfall, unless we split up, one watchin' the
front, one watchin' the back, he'll sneak out and ride
that horse across the Rio Grande and never be seen
again in these parts."

"You're packin' a star, too, Bob. Why don't you call
him out? Tell him we won't hurt him if he comes peace-
able."

"Last man I called out come a runnin' with both pistols blazin'. Liked to have parted my hair before I
dropped him with a belly shot."

"Jesus, Bob."

"Well, I'm tellin' you this, Talley is one bad hombre.
He's a-watchin' us right now and if he's any shot at all,
he can drop us if we let our horses take one step more
in his direction."

"So it's a Mexican standoff. We wait him out. You in
back, me in the front, or vice versa."

"It's your call, Brad. But I've got a better idea."

"I'm listening."

"You 'member them Apaches we tracked six months
ago?"

"Yeah."

"We shot their horses out from under them."

"Yeah, Bob, and then they hit the ground and dis-appeared."

"Slithered away like a bunch of lizards."

"In all directions. They plumb gave us the slip."

"Oh, we could have tracked them down. One by one. But they knew what they were doing. They became part of the land and if we'd gotten close to one, we never would have seen him until it was too late."

"Yeah, that's what you told me, Bob. Which was why we didn't go after them."

"I said you could be looking right at an Apache and never see him."

"Uh-huh. As long as they weren't moving, they'd look like everything else, a bush, a plant, a rock."

"Well, we're going to get Talley the same way. Sort of."

"I don't follow you, Bobby. He's in there. We know that. He can't hide, but he can shoot us if we go in."

"Not if he can't see us."

"You mean we're going to crawl on our bellies down there? We'd still be moving. He'd see us."

"Not if he doesn't know where to look. Now, here's the way I see it, Brad. We'll turn our horses and ride off. Just like we was givin' up. Let Talley think we went back into Del Rio to get drunk or whip up a posse, or get help."

"Yeah?"

"I'll get off my horse and crawl back here. Real slow. Inch by inch. Meantime, you ride a wide circle around to the back. You take your time, so I can crawl up there with my rifle and turn invisible."

"And?"

"And you'll leave your horse before you get the back of the adobe in sight. You crawl up on your belly to a spot within range of Talley's horse. Then you shoot the horse and be real still. I figure he'll either come out the front or run to the back to see what the shooting's about.

When he first sees that horse, his horse, his dead horse, that's all he'll see. Then I'll either shoot him in the front of the adobe or you'll shoot him when he comes out back to see about his poor old dead horse."

"Christ, Wakefield, that's the dumbest idea I've ever heard in my whole life."

"If you have a better one," Wakefield said, "let's hear it."

"Your idea might work. If we kill Talley's horse, he might surrender."

"He might."

"I am bound to apprehend him, Bob."

"I know."

"Alive."

"If you can, Brad."

"Apprehend. Not kill."

Wakefield shrugged.

Two hours later, Talley's horse lay dead in back of the adobe.

"Talley, this is Captain Brad Chambers of the Texas Rangers. If you surrender to me, you will not be hurt."

Talley emerged from the adobe and started shooting with two pistols.

Bob Wakefield had moved to another position, to the side of the adobe. He took careful aim with his rifle and shot Talley in the head. Talley dropped, dead before he hit the ground.

"Bob, you could have shot him in the leg."

"Brad, that boy would have been trouble. He didn't aim to leave that adobe alive."

"Well, shit, Bob."

"I know. He wanted to take one or both of us with him. He didn't want to be apprehended, don't you think?"

"I guess not, Bob. Damn."

"Let's go untie those poor Mexicans, Brad. Maybe you'll feel better."

"Brad?"

"Huh?"

"You daydreamin'?" Randy asked.

"No. I, uh, was just trying to get a rope on what Thorne might be thinking. He seems to be a very careful man."

"Yeah. Well, if we're ever going to catch him, we'd better keep after him."

"You're right. I'll take the point, you take up the rear. Paco, you take the right flank, Gid, the left."

"Back to a military formation, eh, Major?" Lou asked. "Where do you want me?"

"I want you to scout ahead of me, Lou."

"Why not Randy? He knows the country better'n I do."

"I want fresh eyes up there. If you're not familiar with any of the terrain you're not likely to be fooled."

"What am I looking for?" Lou asked.

"That pack horse and the man who stayed behind to listen for us. Thorne may try to protect his rear. If you see anybody who doesn't belong on this road, don't get in a fight. Either fire off a round from your rifle or pistol, or come hell-for-leather back to me and report."

"Yes, sir, Major sir."

Brad didn't reply to Lou's sarcastic affirmation, but lifted his hand and dropped it to signal his men to get moving.

They rode for two more hours. Brad read the signs that told him the man who had stayed behind to check on them had caught up to the others. He was now tracking just three men and they were not dawdling.

Fifteen minutes later, Randy rode up from the rear.

"Brad, Lou must have found the path that goes to the Cooper place. It's right up yonder, close to the creek we passed a while back."

"Better go up and see if you can find Lou. Tell him to wait."

Randy did not reply, but galloped on ahead and disappeared from view. Brad called in Paco and Gid from the flanks. "We'll stick together for a time," Brad told them.

"Where'd Randy go?" Gid asked.

"We're close to the Cooper place. He went ahead to find Lou."

A few minutes later, Brad saw the path Randy had told him about. He turned onto it, then stopped and looked closely at the ground. There was a veritable maze of tracks, hoofprints upon hoofprints, coming and going, each obliterating another. And there, atop those of the men they were chasing, were the tracks of Lou's and Randy's horses, each going only one way—down the wide path, through the thick woods.

A second later, Brad stiffened when a single gunshot pierced the silence. It came from beyond the trees and Brad's stomach churned as the sound hung in the air like the lingering aftertones of a death knell.

17

BRAD'S STOMACH TURNED WHEN HE SAW THE BODIES of the man and the woman lying in the garden. Lou and Randy were afoot, standing next to the dead people. Lou had his rifle, the butt braced against his knee, and Brad knew it was he who had fired the shot that brought him, Paco, and Gid riding in at a gallop.

"These are the Coopers," Randy said, with a wave of his hand. "Or used to be."

Brad knew they were dead without asking. He dismounted and walked into the garden. Gid and Paco stayed on their horses, their faces drawn and pale.

"They never had a chance," Lou said, his voice tinged with a bitter edge.

"They had a mule," Randy said. "It's gone. Tracks of it, though. And tracks of someone else who was here. I reckon after they were killed."

Brad looked at the faces of the dead people. He could not help thinking what the war had done to Texas and other places. As slaves, these two would have still been alive, but not free. As free people, they had given up their lives. It was all so sad, so utterly sad and unnecessary. These people had done nothing to anyone. They had not caused the Civil War, nor fought in it. They looked at peace now, but the blood on them attested to the violence of their deaths.

"It's not pretty," Randy said.

"No, it's very ugly," Brad said, and scuffed the heel of his boot across a furrow.

"They were good people," Randy said.

Brad walked over and examined the ground around the bodies. Then he followed the small footprints until they left the garden. He saw the sign that told him more about what had happened.

"Mule was brought here through those trees," Brad said. "A small person, a girl, probably, led it here and then led it back. Where does that path go, Randy?"

"Probably to the Worth place. It's not far if you walk through those trees. The road leads to a crossroads and the right branch goes to the Worth place."

"We'll split up," Brad said. "Any idea who these small footprints might belong to?"

"Norm Worth has a couple of kids. A boy and a girl. Gal's name is Hollie. Boy is named Cal."

Brad turned to Gid. "See if you can find a shovel in the barn, Gid. Paco, find a shady spot where the ground is soft. I want these people buried proper."

Paco dismounted before Gid. He led his horse to a tree on the edge of the garden and tied it up, then started looking around for a burial place. Gid rode to the barn, tied his horse to a hitch ring on a post, and went inside. He returned with two shovels.

"Randy and Lou, why don't we ride through the woods yonder and see if we can find any of the Worths. Ask them if they know what happened here."

"I don't like what I'm feelin'," Randy said.

"Neither do I," Brad replied.

Lou caught up his horse and rode toward the path that led through the woods, where he waited for Brad and Randy. Paco and Gid were already digging a double grave under the shade of a live oak.

"Gid, when you're finished, you and Paco ride through the woods to the Worth place. Keep your eyes open."

"We will," Gid said. "You want 'em deep or shallow?"

"Deep enough to keep the critters from digging them up," Brad said. "And," he added, "see you treat 'em decent."

"Will do, Major," Gid said, touching two fingers to his hat brim.

"Lead out, Randy," Brad said, after Randy had caught up his horse and mounted. They joined Lou and headed into the forest.

Brad studied the tracks on the path through the woods. He saw where the girl had led the mule from the Cooper farm, then back again. So, he thought, she must have either seen them get killed, or come upon them just after they were shot.

"Smoke ahead," Randy called.

Brad looked up and saw the columns of smoke. His stomach seemed to fall inside him as if he had stepped into a hole and dropped a foot or two.

"Not much smoke," he said.

"Smells of wood," Lou said.

"Yeah, wood smoke," Randy said, as he wound through the trees: hickory and oak, a few willows, some mesquite, sumac.

Finally, Randy rode into a clearing, and beyond, the three men saw a house and barn, with three thin columns of smoke rising from a field they could not see over the slight rise the land made beyond their line of vision.

"That's Worth's place," Randy said. "Looks peaceful enough."

"He must be burnin' stumps," Lou said.

Brad said nothing, but looked all around as far as he could see. Randy set a course for the house, with Lou behind him and Brad in the rear.

"That don't smell like just wood smoke no more," Lou said, crinkling his nose.

Brad nodded. "It smells like . . ." And then his stomach turned and bile rose up in his throat, gagging him.

The three riders topped the rise and the field where the stumps were burning came into view. That was when they heard the distinct sound of someone sobbing.

Randy turned away from the house and started toward the open field. Lou and Brad caught up with him and they rode side by side in silence.

"That looks like Hollie Worth yonder," Randy said, pointing to a figure bending over something in the field. The stench of burning flesh was strong in their nostrils now, mingled with the wood smoke, and Lou held his nose, grimaced, as they rode ever closer.

"Oh, Cal, oh my God." The woman's voice carried on the still air and sent shivers up Brad's spine.

"Hollie," Randy called out. "Hollie, it's me, Randy Dunn, from over to Cottonwood Creek."

The woman, no more than a girl to Brad's eyes, looked up, shielding her eyes from the sun with her right hand. She seemed dazed, Brad thought, or addled. There was a bewildered expression on her face.

"Randy? Is that you?"

"Yeah, Hollie. With some friends. What happened here?"

"Oh, God, Randy, they killed everybody—Pa, Cal, the Coopers . . . "

"Did you see 'em?" Randy asked, swinging off his horse.

"No, I just heard shots. I just heard shots and now they're dead, oh God."

Brad slipped out of the saddle. Lou stayed mounted when Brad put up a hand. He nodded as Brad handed him the reins to his horse and followed Randy into the field.

"Brad, this is Hollie Worth," Randy said. "Hollie, this is my old cavalry boss, Major Brad Chambers."

"It's just Brad."

"Look what they've done, Randy. Poor Pa. Poor Cal."

Cal's clothing was scorched and still smoldering. Brad saw where Hollie had dragged his body away from one of the burning stumps.

"I'm real sorry, ma'am," Brad said, taking off his hat out of respect. "We know who did this and we mean to bring them to justice."

"That's why we're here," Randy said.

"You mean you know these men?" Hollie asked.

"No'm," Brad said, "we don't know them. But we've been charged with catching them and taking them before a court of law."

"You ought to shoot them dead," Hollie said. Her clothes were smeared with dirt and there was soot and ashes on her face. But Brad saw that she was a comely woman, probably in her early twenties, with wet blue eyes and auburn hair, and a figure that could not be hidden under the loose clothing she wore: a pair of dyed cotton trousers and a faded chambray shirt, with flat-soled boots that laced up to the high tops, much like the brogans on her brother's feet.

"Can you tell us what happened?" Brad asked.

"They shot Cal over by the house, and dragged him over here and threw him on a burning stump. They shot my pa in the barn and dragged him here, too. Both of them were on top of stumps. Why?"

"I reckon they're just mean men, Hollie," Randy said.

"They killed the Coopers, too," she said. "Shot them both down in cold blood."

"We know," Brad said. "Two of my men are burying them now."

"Oh, my God," she said. "I never thought about that. And I've got to bury my pa and my brother."

"We'll do it for you," Brad said.

Hollie brushed her brother's face tenderly, then leaned down and kissed him on the forehead. She stood up, tears brimming in her eyes. "I—I don't think I could bear putting them in the ground myself. I'd like to wash them up, though. Put some clean clothes on Daddy and Cal."

"We'll help you, Hollie," Randy said. "Do you want us to carry them out back to the pump?"

"Yes, I—I guess that would be best." She glanced down at her own clothes. "Well, look at me, will you? I look like I've been wallowing with the hogs." She brushed back a vagrant strand of burnished hair that had fallen over her dirty face. "I look a mess."

"You look just fine, Hollie," Randy said. "Considerin'."

"I—I'll just go on to the house. Will you . . . will you bring Pa and Cal around back?"

"We'll do it, ma'am," Brad said. "Will you be all right?"

"Do you mean am I going to cry again? Probably. I just don't want anybody to see me when I do."

She broke into a sob then and started running toward the house, her man's shirt flopping its tail, her boots making soft sounds on the earth.

"Poor gal," Randy said. "She put a lot of store in her pa. Her brother wasn't quite right in the head, but she was like a mother to him."

"What about her mother?" Brad asked.

"She died some time back. Hollie's had a lot on her shoulders. And now this."

Brad sighed. He looked at the two dead men and shook his head. Suddenly, none of that day seemed real. There were too many dead and Thorne was making tracks to parts unknown, putting more distance between himself and his pursuers. But he couldn't just ride off and leave these messes for one lone girl to clean up.

This was looking more and more like the war he had thought was over. Dead people everywhere and so senseless. But this was a different war. The dead had had no chance to defend themselves, and they had not been at war. They were innocent victims of a madman—

and the more Brad thought about it, the more convinced he became that Thorne was mad, an insane killer with no conscience.

Lou dismounted, led the horses to a bush, and tied the reins loosely to the branches. He and Randy picked up Norm Worth, Randy by the shoulders, Lou by the dead man's feet. Brad shouldered Cal's body, surprised at its lightness. The corpse was starting to stiffen, but was not fully into rigor mortis. He followed Randy and Lou to the pump behind the house, where the two men laid out Norm. Brad gently placed Cal's body beside his father's. Hollie must have closed their eyes because they were tightly shut, which made it slightly easier to look at them. Brad shook his head again.

"So damned senseless," he said.

"Who in hell is Abel Thorne?" Randy asked. "Is he plumb crazy? I think Grimley's got a lot to answer for, too. No government gave him the right to kill anybody for not paying taxes."

"You think that's why these two men were killed?" Lou asked.

Randy fished out his makings and began building a smoke. He offered the sack to Lou, who took it and fished in his pocket for papers. When he had built his, he handed the tobacco sack to Brad, who built a quirly and held it to the match Randy lit.

"Grimley might be just somebody Thorne's using for his own purposes," Brad said, blowing a spume of blue smoke out of his mouth. "The papers he served you two looked legitimate."

"Yeah, they did," Randy said. "I just can't figure out why Thorne's doing all this. Does he want land? He's doing it the hard way, seems to me."

"Thorne is a man just plumb full of hate," Brad said. "Blind hate. I've seen it before in such men. Men like Thorne are cowards at heart. They pick on weaker people, unsuspecting people. Their hate is so strong, they'll use any excuse to kill. Thorne is like a man who kicks his dog. At first he may kick it for a reason. But after that, he just enjoys kicking the dog. It makes him feel like a big man, a strong man to kick that dog."

"Yeah, I've known men like Thorne," Randy said. "I thought Colonel Ford was that way until I got to know him."

"No, Rip was not that way," Brad said. "He's a decent man. Thorne is like a pox on the land. He infects everything he touches."

"I'd like to infect him," Lou said. "With lead poisoning."

"I say rope and drag the son-of-a-bitch," Randy said.

"Go see if you can find some shovels, Randy," Brad said. "Lou, you go and help him. Try the barn."

The two men walked off toward the barn, both still talking about what they'd like to do to Abel Thorne.

Hollie emerged from the house. She was dressed in clean clothes: a pair of sturdy duck pants, a clean man's shirt, and the same boots. Her face was freshly scrubbed and her hair was tied high in the back with a green ribbon, giving her a saucy look. But there was no mistaking the sadness in her eyes.

"The boys have gone to fetch shovels, ma'am," Brad said.

"My name is Hollie. 'Ma'am' is for old schoolteachers."

"Yes'm."

"I'm going with you, you know," she said.

"What?"

"When you go after those men. I'm going with you."

"No, you sure aren't."

"You can't stop me. I can ride and shoot as well as any man and I want to see those men who killed my pa, my brother, and the Coopers."

"You can see 'em in jail."

"I'll see them hanged, or shot," she said, her eyes flashing with determination.

"This is a military expedition, Miss Hollie. No place for a woman. It's very dangerous."

"Living here was dangerous for my pa and my brother. Not to mention those poor Coopers."

"It's not the same. You can't come with us."

"Well, I am, sir, no matter what you say. Where you go, I will go. Until those men are caught or killed."

Brad glared at her, but she stood straight, returning his stare, her chin slightly uptilted, her eyes narrowed to burning slits that seemed to bore right through him.

That's when he twisted his head suddenly, thinking he saw the men out of the corner of his eye. But it was only that shadow that seemed to be following him, vanished now, and the men were still in the barn looking for shovels.

He rubbed his eyes, as if to clear them. When he looked back at Hollie, she was staring at him with an odd expression on her face.

"Did you think you saw someone?" she asked.

Brad shook his head, but he looked over his shoulder again one more time. Just to make sure.

18

GRIMLEY WAS SWEATING HARD, AND NOT JUST FROM the heat of the sun. For two days they had been traveling southwest, with no sign of the man pulling the pack horse since they left the crossroads near the Worth place. He kept expecting to rendezvous with the old man and the pack horse at any moment, but they had traveled miles at a good clip without seeing a soul. They hadn't stopped at any of the farms on his list, either.

Grimley realized that without Abel Thorne, he was completely blind. He had relied on the man to take him to those farms where taxes were owed, and he had served notice on a few. The ones where he had been sent away only to hear gunshots were the ones that weighed heavily on his conscience. He was pretty sure that the Coopers had been shot, and they didn't owe any taxes. He didn't know about the Worths, for sure, but he had heard shots and when he'd asked Thorne about them, he had just taken the papers and said he'd deliver them later. Which was not entirely legal. But he was genuinely afraid of Thorne now, although he had seemed nice enough when they had first met and Thorne had volunteered to show him where all those farms in arrears

were located. Then the old man and Thorne's two hench-
men had joined them and everything had changed from
then on.

"Where are we going, Abel?" Grimley finally asked,
as he wiped his face with a large blue kerchief that was
already stiff with perspiration.

"West," Thorne said.

"I can see that. Any particular place? I still have no-
tices to serve in this general area."

"Hogg's Wells," Thorne said. "We'll get to your no-
tices once we resupply."

"I'm not entirely happy with the way things have been
going. I am not used to the hostility from the landowners. And I should have served Norman Worth."

"You don't have to worry none about Worth."

"What do you mean, sir?"

"I mean he won't give you no more trouble, Grimley.
Ever."

Grimley felt a shiver course up his spine, as if a spider
had crawled up his bare back.

"I cannot and will not be a party to murder, Mr.
Thorne."

"Murder? Why do you say that?"

"Because I suspect that you and your companions
might be murdering landowners."

"Where did you get that idea?"

"I've heard you shooting. And I've not been called in
to serve papers at those places where you fired your
guns."

"Grimley, do you know what your problem is?"

"I'm not aware of any problem beyond my suspicions."

"You think too damned much. Just mind your own
business and we'll get along."

"I am trying to mind my own business, sir. But you
are making it very difficult for me to conduct it prop-
erly."

"Have you collected any taxes yet, Grimley?"

"You know I have not."

"And, you ain't goin' to, neither. These people are dirt poor. They don't have any cash. The damned Yankees came down here and tore up the state and stole our cotton, our tobacco, our food crops, and I don't know what all. The federal government is just a land-grabbin' thief sendin' you down here to collect taxes."

"I thought you were on our side, Mr. Thorne."

"I ain't on nobody's side, Grimley. I just don't believe in free niggers, that's all. Niggers was born to be slaves and anybody who sets 'em free is a damned traitor to Texas."

"I have nothing to do with slavery, sir. It's not my job to enforce the Emancipation Proclamation."

"That's good, Grimley, because if that was your job, I'd shoot you dead right here and now."

Thorne rode away from Grimley, leaving him to tag along in the rear of the three men he had come to distrust. He coughed at the dust Thorne's horse kicked up and wiped his face again with the sweat-stiff kerchief. His clothes were soggy from the boiling sun and he felt as if he must weigh five hundred pounds with all the sweat on him.

It was a two-day ride to Hogg's Wells and Grimley felt isolated from the others at each stop. He kept wondering when they would meet up with the man leading the pack horse, but they never did. Rations were short, and Grimley's belly was growling in protest by the time they reached the wells. It was no more than a way station, and once Thorne and his men watered their horses, they rode on, south of the settlement. Grimley had no choice but to water his horse, fill his canteen, and follow them.

Thorne and his men rode down a slope and entered a heavy thicket of trees at the bottom of the draw. A thin veil of blue smoke hung over the trees and Grimley smelled food cooking. Beef. His stomach roiled with hunger and his mouth began to fill with saliva.

Grimley rode down into the bottom and entered the thicket at the place where he had last seen Thorne and his partners. The smell of food grew stronger and the air was laced with wisps of smoke. He heard the rumble of voices and guffaws of laughter. He rode on toward the aromas and the noises and saw the creek through a gap in the trees, and several men standing up and looking at the three who had just ridden in. Something like fear formed a ball in Grimley's stomach and he felt a sinking feeling in his heart.

He rode into the camp and his gaze swept over the swarm of men, many of them bearded and disheveled, some wearing Confederate trousers or shirts. All were armed, heavily armed, and they turned, as one, and looked at him with dark hooded eyes. Grimley felt as if he had wandered into a nest of snakes.

"Men, this is old Grimley," Thorne said, "a Union carpetbagger come down from Washington to collect taxes from the poor Texians. You look hungry, Grimley. Want something to eat? That's prime beef on the spit yonder. Don't know if the taxes have been paid on it, though."

Grimley saw the fire, then, under a beef carcass run through with a thick willow pole, a man standing beside it, slowly turning it so that it would cook evenly. Atop another fire stood a blackened kettle full of boiling water. Steam rose from the kettle and it carried the aroma of cooked onions and yams or potatoes. Grimley's stomach swirled with hunger pangs, but the ball of fear was still there and he feared he might start to shiver.

"I *am* a bit hungry," Grimley said, and the men all laughed. All except Thorne, who pointed to him.

"From the looks of that belly, Grimley, you ain't gone hungry much," Thorne said.

The men laughed again.

"Light down, Grimley," Thorne said, "and get you a plate. The boys will take care of your horse. Pa, give old Grimley a plate and a fork."

Grimley followed Thorne's gaze and saw the man who had led the pack horse for all those miles.

"That's your father?" Grimley asked Thorne.

"Why, shore, didn't I introduce you? That's Blackjack Thorne, my pa. That don't keep him from callin' me a bastard from time to time."

The men roared with laughter and Thorne swung out of the saddle. Grimley dismounted and waddled over to Blackjack, who reached down and picked up a tin plate and a fork from a number of dishes and utensils he had laid out on a saddle blanket.

"Eat hearty, Grimley," Blackjack said.

More laughter from the others there, as if they all shared the same dark secret.

Blackjack appeared to be very old. He was thin and wiry and bore some resemblance to his son, Abel. Grimley had seen him only once or twice and never up close. It was odd, he thought, that Thorne had never mentioned that the drover was his own father.

"Thanks," Grimley said, taking the plate and fork. Both had been scrubbed with sand, not washed with water, but he felt this was no time to be fastidious. The plate was covered with a thin patina of dust and the fork still had small portions of dried food stuck between the tines.

Herbert Luskin and Orville Trask came up beside Grimley. One of them slapped him on the back. Trask.

"Hurry up, Grimley," Trask said, "or we'll beat you to the trough. Blackjack, better give Grimley two forks."

Blackjack didn't laugh, but he looked quizzically at Grimley, then winked at him. "I think he'll do all right with one fork from what I've seen," Blackjack said.

"Oh, he does all right without no fork at all, I reckon," Trask said. "Don't you, Grimley?"

"I can't help it if I'm stout," Grimley said.

"Stout? Why you're a regular pork barrel, Grimley. Must be the food in Washington. It goes right to your butt and your gut."

The two men laughed, reached down, and picked up plates from the horse blanket. Blackjack handed them forks and they followed Grimley over to the spit, where Abel was now standing with his knife in his hand—a Bowie knife with a huge blade and sharp edges on both sides.

"What do you want, Grimley?" Thorne asked. "A chunk of brisket? Roast?"

"Just anything," Grimley replied, his mouth watering.

"I'll cut you off a good chunk."

Thorne nodded to the man turning the spit, who stopped pulling on the makeshift handle made from a wagon hub and a spoke. Thorne cut a large piece from the rump of the steer. He grabbed the fork out of Grimley's hand and speared the meat; then, stabbing the other side with his knife, he slabbed the meat onto Grimley's plate.

"Enough? You want more?"

"That is more than adequate, Mr. Thorne. Thank you."

"Go on over to that pot and get yourself some turnips and onions, some taters."

Grimley turned away and walked to the kettle, where a man was waiting with a ladle in his hand. "Bring your plate in close," the man said.

Grimley pushed his plate close to the kettle and the man dipped the ladle in the boiling water and came up with cut potatoes, little wild onions, and what looked to be turnip greens. The man piled Grimley's plate full and Grimley held up his hand as the man started to dip the ladle back into the kettle.

"That's fine, thank you."

"You're more'n welcome to more, pilgrim," the man said, grinning with a set of broken and carious teeth.

Grimley stepped away from the kettle and the fire beneath it that made him perspire even more freely than when he had been riding in the blazing sun. He looked around for a place to sit and eat his meal. He looked to the left and saw the pack horses owned by the men in the camp, and to the right, there was a clot of men just standing in a bunch staring straight at him.

Then Thorne called out to him.

"Over here, Grimley, by the creek. There's a log to sit on. Big enough for your fat ass."

Grimley winced, but walked over and surveyed the rotting log that lay above the creek bank. Thorne waved him to sit down. The other two men who had ridden with Thorne took up places on either end and began eating, forking food into their mouths as if they were starving.

Grimley sat down and sighed heavily. He took out a small pocket knife, opened it and, holding down the chunk of meat, began to slice off one end.

Grimley's head was bent over as he began to devour the food on his plate. He listened to the clank and clatter of utensils as Thorne's men ate their food, and then he heard the shuffle of many feet. He swallowed a mouthful of food and looked up to see Thorne standing in front of him. But he was not alone. Most of the men in camp were there, too, flanking Thorne, and they were all staring at him with blank expressions on their faces.

The food in Grimley's throat stuck halfway down. He choked and Thorne stepped forward and slapped him on the back to dislodge the particles.

"Now, you don't want to go and choke yourself to death, Grimley," Thorne said.

Grimley got the food down and gasped for air. He spluttered and drew out his kerchief and dabbed at his mouth.

"Food good, Grimley?"

"Fair to middling," Grimley said.

"Glad you like it, because it's your last meal."

"What?"

"Well, now, I think you heard me. This is as far as you go. I can serve them papers now that I see how it's done. We don't need no carpetbagger settlin' matters here in Texas, do we, boys?"

The men all grunted and shook their heads.

"Sir, I've been duly sworn . . ."

"Just shut up, Grimley," Thorne said. "You see all these men here? They never surrendered and they were never beaten in your goddamned Civil War. You come down here with your duly sworn and think you can grab land that ain't your'n and just hand it over to the Yankee government. Well, by Judas, you ain't goin' to serve no more papers."

"I'll have to report this, Thorne. You have no authority . . ."

"No authority?" Thorne spat. "I've got twenty cannon that're my authority. That's what these boys come here for. When the last battle was fought at Palmito Hill, my boys run cannon over the border and we aim to pick 'em up, run 'em overland, and blow hell out of ever' exslave we can find. There won't be no freed slaves in Texas, by God, and you can put that in your pipe and smoke it, mister."

"Why, that's murder, Thorne. The U.S. Army will hunt you down and . . ."

"They're already huntin' us, Grimley, and we hope they catch up to us after we get those cannon. Too bad you won't be around to see it."

Grimley's face drained of blood as Thorne drew his pistol.

"No," Grimley said, "you're not . . ."

Thorne swiped him across the face with the pistol barrel. Blood shot from Grimley's nose like juice from a smashed tomato. He reeled back, throwing up his hands, and screamed with the pain. His plate slid off his lap and upended, spilling the food all over the ground.

Through wet eyes, he saw Thorne raise his pistol and level it at his forehead.

"No, please God, no," Grimley said, "don't—don't shoot me . . ."

Grimley saw Thorne's thumb cock the hammer, saw the cylinder of the six-gun spin and stop. He could see the blunt lead in the cylinders that were visible. Then he sucked in a breath as Thorne's index finger curled around the trigger.

"Please," Grimley mewed, his voice a thin squeak.

Then he saw Thorne's finger tighten on the trigger and he heard the explosion, felt the sting of burning powder and the hammerblow of the lead ball as it struck his forehead and then there was only the blackness and the eternal silence.

19

Lieutenant Jared Coy stared at the two fresh graves, with the dirt piled high atop them, beneath the shade of an overhanging oak bough. His tracker, Sergeant Fred Benson, was stalking back and forth across the garden, while his other man, Corporal David Wilkins, watered their horses at a trough near the barn.

"Place is deserted, sir," Wilkins called out.

"But they've been here," Coy said. "Was there anybody in the house?"

"No, sir. Empty, sir." Wilkins led the horses back to the edge of the garden.

"Sergeant?" Coy turned away from the graves and slapped his gloves against his thigh.

"Plenty of tracks, Lieutenant. Two days old, at least."

"Find out which way Chambers went."

"Oh, I know where he went, sir," Benson said. "Right through yonder." He pointed to the woods on the other side of the garden. "But they's mule tracks here, horse tracks, tracks of a small person, a girl, maybe, and a couple probably belong to whoever's buried in them two graves."

"You're sure Chambers was here?"

"Yes, sir, him and them others. They buried some people here and rode off through yonder."

"Mount up," Coy ordered, as he walked toward his horse. Wilkins handed him the reins. He was pulling a pack mule that he had not let water. He'd had nothing but trouble with it the whole trip, and this was his way of asserting his authority. The mule had brayed mightily as the horses drank, but was now just getting ready to balk as it always did when they first started out.

"You going to water that mule, Corporal?" Coy asked.

"Not yet, sir. Look at his belly. He drinks like a camel."

"Just so he doesn't founder along the way."

"Sir, that mule's plumb bloated from the last watering hole."

"Lead out, Sergeant," Coy said, as Benson took to the saddle.

Coy studied the map he'd dug out of his pocket. He had been keeping track of their route. His horse had thrown a shoe the morning before and had put them miles behind Brad Chambers. Sergeant Benson had had to build a fire and perform blacksmith duties by the creek. He had muttered and grumbled, but finally got the shoe reshaped, the hoof trimmed, and the iron nailed to the horse's foot. Coy cursed himself for not bringing extra horses, but he knew if he had, he'd fall further behind Chambers.

He knew by now that Chambers was tracking his quarry, Abel Thorne and four other men. According to Benson, those men were pulling a pack horse and the drover left them every so often to rendezvous further along their route. It was puzzling, thus far, but he felt he was gaining on Chambers, having lost only a day after they left the Dunn place, which he had dutifully marked on his map, as well.

They passed through the woods and came upon another farm, which also appeared deserted. They rode in with rifles at the ready, just in case. But it was very quiet, and Coy knew why, a few moments later, when Benson pointed out two more fresh graves.

"What in hell's going on here, Sergeant?" Coy asked.

"Looks to me like maybe Thorne is killin' every sod-buster he comes across."

"We don't know who is buried in those graves," Coy said. "Maybe Chambers killed Thorne or some of his men."

"We'll soon find out," Benson said. "I'll sort out these tracks and give you a report directly."

"Wilkins," Coy said. "Water that mule. That's an order."

The mule had started braying the minute it smelled water in the trough behind the house.

"Yes, sir," Wilkins said, and pulled on the rope hitched to the mule's bridle.

Coy dismounted and walked up to the house. He called first, then knocked on the door. It was locked. He walked around, peering through the windows, but saw no sign of life. Puzzled, he sat down on the porch, pulled out his pipe, and filled it with tobacco. He lit it and watched Benson walk around the place. He noticed the burning stumps, which gave the illusion that the inhabitants of the farm were close by. But he knew they weren't.

By the time Coy had finished his pipe, Benson was finished deciphering the maze of tracks. He walked over to the house and stood in the shade of the porch roof, one foot on the bottom step.

"Well, Sergeant?" Coy asked.

"Two fresh graves out back of the house. No animals in the barn, but it appears they were turned out to pasture, except for one horse. There's fairly fresh manure in one stall. A day old, maybe. Piss smells."

"Spare me those details, please," Coy said.

"Chambers lit a shuck, is all I know. He's got a new rider, a girl, I figure, or maybe a boy."

"What makes you think it might be a girl?"

"Tracks could be either. Small person. But I found long strands of hair stuck to the stall, kind of coppery, silky hair. Could be a woman's, or a boy with long hair. And I smelled a whiff of perfume in the barn."

"Perfume?"

"Yes, sir, stronger than lilac water. Flowery, but stronger than any flower gives off. Perfume, I'd say. Made me homesick for Kentucky."

Coy arose from the chair.

"Go tell Wilkins to shake a leg. We have some riding to do."

"Sir, what is this Chambers to you? I mean, I know you're supposed to be tracking him and watching him, but I wondered if you knew him or maybe had a grudge against him."

"Benson, that's really none of your business. But, no, I don't know the man. Phil Sheridan picked him to go after this Abel Thorne. I don't know why. General Granger sent me to check on Chambers. Why do you ask?"

"Well, I seem to remember a Chambers that rode with Colonel Ford and that damned Cavalry of the West. He chased us out of the Rio Grande Valley."

"Who were you with?" Coy asked.

"I was temporarily assigned to Vidal's Raiders. Partisans. Shit duty."

"I was with Ed Davis's little cavalry outfit."

"Then you know what that bastard Ford was like down there."

"He gave us fits," Coy said, and he looked off into the distance as he remembered that odd time when Colonel Ford's Cavalry of the West was engaged in guerrilla warfare; when he almost seemed like a ghost.

It was in '62, and the land was parched dry all through the Rio Grande Valley. Davis figured Ford would be hard-pressed to gather together any sizable cavalry, and if he did, he'd have hard forage.

But Ford fooled everybody in the Union forces, the bastard.

Ford had a lot of cavalrymen to start with, but no way to assemble them, so he had them scattered all along the Rio Grande and through the valley. He couldn't find forage and he couldn't mount a military campaign. But he found forage in Mexico and finally was able to assemble a small cavalry unit of 400 horses. He ordered his captains to roll up the Union garrisons. He cut lines of communication. His captains roamed in and out of the thick border brush and laid ambushes in the ebonal. They floated through the chaparral like wraiths cutting Union supply lines and communications.

The young Union troops were mostly infantry and no match for Ford's strike-and-disappear tactics. The Yankee kids were sweating in the hot tropical sun that was almost unbearable at times. They were outfought and outnumbered.

Davis's cavalry fought well, and so did Vidal's Raiders, but they were no match for Ford, who had superior mobility and a cunning that defied Union military minds.

Vidal's force consisted mainly of confederate deserters, like Benson, while Davis's small outfit was just outclassed from the very beginning. Every time they found one of Ford's units, they were beaten back or lost contact in the thick brush. It was a nightmare.

He caught glimpses of Major Brad Chambers now and then. And that tracker, Bob Wakefield. Sometimes Chambers acted as a scout and would come upon them by surprise. When Davis sent men to chase after him, he would just vanish. Some of the others in the outfit thought Chambers, and Ford, too, for that matter, was superhuman. Brad was as bold as Ford was clever and deceptive. And he was a fighter. Once, Chambers and a small cadre of cavalry caught them from the rear and his attack threw confusion into the ranks. Coy had gotten a good look at him then. He was not a man who sent *his men into battle; he led them, and he didn't wield a saber for show, either, like some line officers. Chambers carried a rifle and pistol and he was a crack shot. He had to admit that during that whole time of drought and tropical rain and heat, Chambers had assumed bigger-than-life proportions.*

In April of that year, the rains finally came, and it did help grow some grass, but it also turned the valley into a steam bath. Davis's men and horses were bathed in sweat and it was difficult to breathe in the steaming thick air.

Ford and his men camped out in the brush for a time when Davis and Vidal were hunting him. They knew he was in there somewhere, but could not find him. Then Ford surprised them all when it rained for ten straight days. Ten days of hot hard rain that turned the valley into slippery mud and blinded Davis and his men, be-wildered Vidal's force.

Ford went on the march, riding straight through the heavy torrential rains toward Ringgold Barracks. His forces easily took Los Angeles, Los Ojuelos, and Co-mitos. He ran the Union infantry out of Rio Grande City without firing a shot. The Union soldiers just saw him and left the city to his cavalry without a fight.

After that brilliant forced march through the constant hellish downpour that nearly drowned the Union forces, Ford gathered his scattered cavalry together and used some to guard his flank, others to screen his front; he rode unopposed right into Mexico to secure his remain-ing flank.

Ford then began confiscating all the cotton ready to ship and he sold the goods for hard cash, silver coin. With the silver, Ford bought rations for his men and then he struck up friendships with all the Mexican com-mandants, forming an alliance with those around Ca-margo. To Davis's dismay, Ford's Mexican friends closed the border to Vidal's Raiders, who had been us-

ing the Rio Grande as a buffer and a protective shield.

Then Ford put a liaison officer with Juan Cortinas. He bought guns from Union deserters in Mexico, and from Cortinas in Matamoros he was able to obtain a cannon.

"That son-of-a-bitch isn't getting any help from the Confederates," Davis told them. "He's doing all this on his own. He's smart as a snakewhip. He's got his own personal army, by God, and the Mexicans are helping him like he was a long-lost brother."

"Sir, Wilkins is here," Benson said.

Coy shook off his thoughts and refocused his eyes. For a long moment, he had been transported back to those days when Ford and Chambers had made them all look like fools.

"I hate Texas, Benson, you know that?" Coy said.

"Sir?"

"I hate this whole goddamned godless place. It's only fit for rattlesnakes and vultures."

"Yes, sir. It's some kind of lonesome place. And this here farm gives me the williwaws, for sure."

Wilkins stood by the mule, holding the reins to his horse in the same hand that held the lead rope. He looked at Coy with a quizzical look on his face.

"It's not just this place, it's all of Texas. It's the wind and the vastness of it, the desolate country that stretches forever; it's the damned rains and the twisters, the snakes and the mosquitoes, the flies and the spiders. It's not a fit place for a man to live. It's a desert, most of it, and the ugliest place I've ever seen."

"I don't like it much, neither," Benson said. "Not like Kentucky. It's too flat and too ornery to suit me."

"I'm glad you agree with me, Benson. Now, let's mount up and go find Chambers. Do you think we can catch him?"

"Sir, I think he knows we're on his trail and if he wants us to catch him, he'll let us. But from what I've heard of him and what little I saw of him when he was riding with Colonel Ford, he can ride into a hole and pull the hole in after him where we'd never see him or find him."

"He's just a man, Benson. Just like you and me."

"I don't know about that, sir. I think sometimes he's got eyes in the back of his head."

"Well, we're going to catch up to him."

"And then what, Lieutenant?"

Coy drew in a deep breath and held it. Then he climbed aboard his horse and looked off into the distance.

"I don't know, Benson. But one reason you're here is that you're a sharpshooter—the best there is."

"You want me to shoot Chambers?"

"It might come to that," Coy said.

"Well, now. I had him in my sights once."

"You did?"

"Down on the Rio. Vidal sent me to do some damage to that reb cavalry. I had Chambers dead in my sights."

"And what happened?"

"Sir, I can't explain it. I was in the brush and my face was smeared with dirt. There was no way he could see me. I was like one of them lizards what holds so still you can't hardly tell it's there."

"And?"

"Chambers, he turned and looked straight at me. I mean his eyes looked right into my eyes and I got a shiver up my back."

"So did you take the shot?"

"Well, sir, Chambers just kind of smiled at me, like he knew I had buck fever, and then he wheeled his horse, ducked low, and before I could swing the barrel on him, he plumb up and disappeared. It wasn't hardly natural."

Coy mounted his horse and snorted.

"He's just a man, Benson. Just a goddamned man, like anybody else."

Then Coy kicked his horse's flanks with his spurs and shot out ahead of his men and they had to ride hard to catch up to him.

20

BRAD KNEW WHERE THORNE WAS HEADED AFTER AN-
other day of tracking him south of the Worth farm. The
irony was not lost on him. Hogg's Wells. A place he
knew well, for he and Colonel Ford had used it as a
hideout when they were conducting guerrilla warfare
against Union troops in the Rio Grande Valley.

"Where are we goin'?" Gid asked, when Brad left the
road and the tracks and started off in another direction.

"Oh, you noticed, did you?"

"Well, I mean, we been follerin' these tracks for better'n a day and . . ."

"Gid, remember I told you about some caches when
we first started out?"

"Yep. I remember you sayin' something about it. Re-
supply."

"Right. Well, that's where we're going and it's right
on our way. We pick up this trail as the road bends back
toward Hogg's Wells."

"That was one of the hideouts we used when we were
chasin' Yankees," Gid said.

"Or when they were chasing us," Brad said.

"What makes you think Thorne will go to Hogg's Wells?"

"Some of the Confederate deserters knew about that place and, after the war was over, I scouted it out and saw men that had a camp there. Men like Abel Thorne."

"So, you're guessin'."

"I'm guessing," Brad said. Then he cocked his thumb and pointed it to the rear. "How's she doing, Gid?"

"Miss Hollie? She's packin' a heap of grief, but she's a trooper. Doesn't mind eatin' dust."

"She doesn't belong here," Brad said.

"None of us belongs here, Major."

Brad turned and looked back toward the rear. Hollie was riding a small horse, a four-year-old bay mare with a blaze face and one white stocking. A rifle jutted from a saddle scabbard and she was packing a .36 caliber Navy Colt percussion pistol. She had a powder horn slung over her shoulder and carried a possibles pouch with lead balls, grease, and percussion caps. Her saddle-bags were full of beef jerky, coffee, sugar, hardtack biscuits, dried beans, and other foodstuffs she'd packed. He had tried his best to talk her out of coming with them, but she was as stubborn as a mule. They had all spent the night at her house and at dawn, she was ready to go.

He turned away just as Hollie caught his glance and lifted a hand in a tentative wave as if to reassure him that she was all right.

"She may be, but I'm sure as hell not."

"What?" Gid asked.

"Nothing," Brad said, glowering as he put spurs to his horse and picked up the pace. Gid dropped back behind him, and Brad rode alone, on the point, pondering ways he might get rid of Hollie Worth.

There was a man waiting for Brad and his friends at Little Thicket, the remnant of a little settlement that had been abandoned shortly after Texas seceded from the Union and war was declared.

"Colonel Chambers," the man said, saluting. "I

brought fresh horses, the rifles, and some pistols and ammunition, as you ordered."

"Who are you?" Brad asked.

"Second Lieutenant Benjamin Ferris, sir."

"Where are your men, Lieutenant?"

"Concealed, sir. One in the livery with your mounts, another in that little shack over there, and two more behind that old lean-to down the street."

"Well done. Call them out, Lieutenant."

"Yes sir," Ferris said, and put two fingers to his lips. He gave three sharp whistles and Union soldiers appeared in the tumbleweed-strewn street. They streamed toward them, rifles in their hands.

"What are your orders, Ferris?" Brad asked.

"Sir, I'm to deliver what we brought and then wait here for an undetermined length of time."

"Why?"

"I'm not at liberty to say, sir."

Brad looked over the young lieutenant. He was barely dry behind the ears, his blond hair trimmed regulation short, the beginning fuzz of a mustache above his upper lip, short sideburns, a peach complexion, and bright blue eyes. His men arrived and stood at attention until Brad ordered them to stand at ease.

"Never mind, Ferris. I know you're to wait here for whoever's been on my tail for the past week."

"I can't say, Colonel," Ferris said.

Brad dismounted and waved to the others to do the same. "If your men will help with the remounts we'll get this over quickly."

"Yes, sir. Horner, you and your men take these people to the stable. Lassiter, take the Colonel to the arms cache."

"You're a colonel, Brad?" Randy asked, as he led his horse and began to follow Private Horner to the stables.

"It's a long story," Brad said.

"Sir, is that a woman with you?" Ferris asked.

"That's another long story, Ferris."

"Yes, sir," Ferris said.

Hollie stopped in front of Brad and Ferris. "I don't want another horse," she said. "I'll ride Bessie here."

"Suit yourself, ma'am," Brad said. "Your horse looks sound enough. But we're going through some rough country."

"Where are you going from here, sir?" Ferris asked.

"I think I'd better keep that to myself, Lieutenant."

Ferris stiffened, but said nothing. Hollie grained her horse in a shady part of the street, using her hat for a feed bag. Brad led his horse to the stables to change mounts. Ferris walked over to where Hollie was standing.

"Ma'am," he said.

"Yes?"

"I'm Ben Ferris. Who might you be, ma'am?"

She told him her first name.

"Do you know the colonel well?" he asked.

"I hardly know him at all. I thought he was a major. That's what the others call him."

"Do you know the others riding with the colonel?"

"I know a couple of them. Why?"

"I was just wondering what you were doing with such men."

"Such men?"

"Well, they're pretty rough and you appear to have some refinement."

"Why thank you, Mr. Ferris, but those men are after the men who murdered my parents and when we catch up to them, I'll be just as rough as they are."

"Yes'm. But this is a military expedition and . . ."

"And you don't think I should be a part of it. Right?"

"Yes'm. It could be dangerous."

"Mr. Ferris, let me tell you something my daddy told me—a long time ago. Livin' in Texas is dangerous. If you don't know that yet, you will. I trust these men I'm with and I don't trust Yankees who speak ill of them."

"Miss Hollie, I wasn't . . . I mean, I didn't . . ."

"I know what you meant, Mr. Ferris. Now, if you don't mind, I'd like to be alone, please. I'm sure you have duties to perform."

"Yes, ma'am, I surely do," Ferris said. He turned and walked away. Hollie stared at his back until he was nearly out of sight. Then she turned away and led her horse behind a ramshackle building that had somehow survived the ravages of wind and rain, but was gradually rotting away, its lumber long since faded to gray, its bricks crumbling to dust.

She let out a sigh and slowly began to weep. That young soldier had reminded her of Cal. Not that they looked anything alike, but Cal could have become like Ferris, a soldier, perhaps, a man with promise, with a future.

But Cal's future had been taken away from him with a single bullet. And how far away was Lieutenant Ferris from the same fate? How far were any of them, for that matter? She had known boys who had gone away to fight in the war, and many had not come back. Cal was spared that, as was her father, but the war had left its poison and men were still dying. It was all so sad, and so hard.

But her daddy had warned her, long ago, that she might have to face life without him, without her brother.

"Texas is hard," he'd told her. "Life is hard, and the only thing you can expect is the unexpected. Your mother died before her time and you've had to take care of me and your brother. You've got to prepare yourself for more hardship before your life is done, Hollie."

She had not wanted to listen to his words, but they came back to her now, and they brought fresh tears to her eyes.

"You were right, Daddy," she said aloud.

Then a shadow fell over her, and she looked up and saw Brad standing there. She began to wipe her face free of tears and dab at her leaking eyes.

"About what?" Brad asked, handing her the kerchief he kept in his pocket.

"It doesn't matter. Are you ready to leave?"

"In a minute. I just wanted one more chance to try to persuade you to go back home. I'm going to order a forced march and it's going to be pretty rough on horses and men."

"I know."

"No, you don't, young lady. These men we're after would as soon kill you as look at you. If you'd been at home when they rode up, we'd have buried you, too."

"I know that, Colonel."

"And don't call me colonel."

"Then don't you call me young lady."

"That's what you are."

"And you're a colonel in the Yankee army, Mr. Chambers."

"Just for this military campaign."

"And then what?"

"I'm a Texas Ranger. I'll go back to doing that. Not that it's any of your business."

"Maybe it is my business," she said, then compressed her lips as if to seal them.

"What do you mean?" he asked.

"Nothing. Just leave me alone. When you're ready to go, just holler. I need some privacy right now."

Brad's face reddened, as she began to unbuckle her belt as if to remove her pants, or to drop them to relieve herself. She turned her back on him as if to conceal what she was doing.

"Oh, I'm real sorry," he said. "I—I'll holler when . . . when . . ."

"Just go, Colonel Chambers."

"Yes'm," he said quickly and walked away, leaving her alone.

Once Brad had gone, Hollie pulled her belt tight and smoothed her trousers in front. She sighed to herself and leaned against the wall for support, closing her eyes.

The trembling started, then, the trembling that had begun, and that she had quelled, when she first caught sight of Lt. Ferris in his Union uniform and became harder to control when the other soldiers came out of hiding.

They came in the night, and when she first heard the hoofbeats and the whickers of the horses, she thought it was her daddy and her brother returning from Galveston, but knew in her heart that it was too soon. She did not expect them for another three days.

She lighted the lamp in the living room, turned up the wick, then ran to the window and looked out. That's when she felt her heart sinking like a stone in her chest. Three men, dressed in Federal blue uniforms, rode up to the front door. She froze by the window when the men looked at her, and even though she could not see their eyes, she could feel the intensity of their stares.

The uniforms were not new and they were not clean. She noticed that, for some reason. The men were not clean-shaven but bearded, and they appeared filthy. Their uniforms appeared frayed and she noticed holes in them and stains that she could not identify.

"Well, looky there," one of the men said.

"You boys just stay put," the leader said as he dismounted.

She stepped away from the window, but she could not make her legs work beyond that one step and she heard the front door open and then the man was in the room. He had a pistol in his hand and he glanced everywhere.

"Hello there, girlie. You're all alone, aintcha?"

"G—go away," her voice squeaked, trapped in a paralyzed throat.

The man laughed and came for her. He grabbed her around the waist and pulled her to him. He bent her head back as he kissed her and she tasted the foul flavor of his mouth and smelled the stench of his rank breath. She felt the blood drain from her brain and grew giddy from his smothering embrace.

He began to rip off her nightgown and she heard the

whisper of his pistol as he sheathed it in his holster. Then, with both hands, he touched her breasts and between her legs and she saw his hideous face in the lamp-glow, smelled the odor of his body as he forced her to the floor, onto her back.

"No, no."

"Shut up, gal. This ain't gonna take long."

There was the creak of his boots as he slipped them from his feet, the thunk of them striking the floor, and the rustle of his trousers as he removed them. He pried her legs apart with his hands and she felt the stab of him before she swooned.

Shadows of the men, as the other two came and took her as she lay in a stupor, the pain a distant piercing, their laughter harsh and muffled to her ears and she heard them call each other by name, but she couldn't decipher them just then, and then she heard them stalking through the house and eating at the table and then the leader was on her again, like an animal, and she saw his face through slitted eyes. The weakness in her legs made her feel as if they were no longer hers and she could not fight, could not rise up from the depths of her befuddled mind, could not regain her senses until he was finished with her and she heard one of the men call out from somewhere she could not fathom.

"Come on, Abe, time's a-wastin'. We got to get movin' again."

Then, the clatter of their boots and the silence afterward and the numbness in her so deep she could not move for a long time, and she drifted in and out of swoon states until daylight streamed through the open door and the window and she broomed the thick cobwebs from her brain and wondered if she had dreamed it all. Wondered that until the pain shook her body and made her crumple up and weep with the shame of it.

She scrubbed and cleaned and dusted and cried and beat her fists against the walls. When her daddy and Cal came back, there was no trace of the men who had vi-

olated her and she managed to smile and stay awake a while longer, for she had not slept through a night since the men had come, but sat with the scattergun on her lap, hoping they would come, hoping they would walk through the door just one more time.

The only name she could remember was "Abe," but the other two were there, just beyond her reach, somewhere on the edges of her mind, all jumbled and incomprehensible. But she knew she would remember their names if she ever heard them uttered again.

"Miss Hollie. Time to go."

Gideon's voice snapped her out of her horrible reverie and she had stopped trembling.

"Coming," she called out, and jerked away from the wall and pulled on the reins of her horse. She walked back out into the sunlight and the soldiers were standing there, watching, as Brad and the others mounted up.

"Ready?" Brad asked her, and she noticed he did not look into her eyes.

"I'm ready," she said and climbed up into the saddle.

She looked at the soldiers one last time as Brad led them out from that place called Little Thicket, and she did not recognize any of their faces. They were all too young and stood too straight.

No, these were not the men who had come in the night so long ago, but they wore the same uniforms, and the memory returned. Hollie shuddered and gritted her teeth as she clapped her spurs to her horse's flanks, mercifully feeling the horse roll beneath her and fall into a trotting gait that would carry her away from the soldiers staring at her, she knew, but not the ones she wanted to kill.

21

BRAD SWORE UNDER HIS BREATH WHEN HE SAW THE body. He was the first to see it, as he had ordered the others to stay back while he rode up to the camp. This was a place he knew well, and he was irritated that Thorne knew about it, too.

He raised his arm and beckoned for the others to come in. The tracks from Hogg's Wells told some of the story, and here, in this abandoned encampment, he saw where they had kept the horses, where they had slept and cooked and eaten. He saw what was left of a roasted steer, mostly skeleton, but with a few pieces of meat still clinging to the bones.

When he had ridden up, a dozen turkey buzzards had taken flight, padding away from the spitted carcass with ungainly legs like aged and desecrated eagles, some with strips of meat still dangling from their beaks. And now they filled the sky, seeking the air currents that would allow them to circle their interrupted meal with the least effort.

Randy was the first to join Brad and his mouth dropped open in surprise.

"Grimley?" Brad asked.

"That's him."

"Certain?"

"No mistake, Major. I'd know that blubber belly anywhere."

Brad pointed to the log. "I figure he was sitting there, maybe gobbling down food, when someone came up to him and put a pistol to his forehead. The buzzards have pretty well picked up all his brains, but there's a chunk lying there from the back of his head."

"Looks like a piece of coconut shell."

"A .44 will do that to a man," Brad said.

"Christ."

Gid and Paco rode up, followed by Lou. Finally, Hollie arrived, but Brad waved her back.

"What is it?" she asked.

"Dead man," Randy said. "The carpetbagger that was riding with Thorne."

"I want to see him," Hollie said.

"It's not pretty, ma'am. He's lyin' faceup in that shallow creek, his eyes picked out by the buzzards and half his head blown away."

"I want to see him," she said, a stubborn undertone to her words.

"Let her," Brad said. "If she gets sick, too damned bad."

Hollie wrestled Bessie up to the creek bank and looked at Grimley's corpse. She gasped and put a fist to her mouth as if to stem the flood of bile that threatened to rise up in her throat.

"Murdered," she said.

"In cold blood," Brad said.

"What do you make of it?" Lou asked. "Thorne killin' him like that."

Brad turned his horse away from the creek and started studying the tracks. "Thorne doesn't need Grimley any more, I reckon. He was just baggage. Look at all these tracks. More than a dozen men were waiting here for him. And they left in a hurry. Heading south."

"Where are they going?" Gid asked.

Brad didn't answer right away. Instead, he began to mull over in his mind just where Thorne might be headed. The ranches in that region were large, encompassing thousands of acres. Thorne would not be so foolish as to visit, or try to take over, such spreads as the King or Falfurrias, nor any of the other huge *estancias* to the south and west. And if he headed east, he would run into heavily traveled roads, many patrolled by Union troops and Texas Rangers.

No, there was only one place Thorne could be headed, and it was so bold and unexpected that Brad began to discern Thorne's reason for returning to the Rio Grande, and not only to the big river, but to a specific place for a specific purpose.

But as Brad brought reason and logic to bear, he realized that the only place Thorne could go and be certain that he could make a stand, or accomplish his purposes, would be that place of death that marked the last battle of the Civil War—Palmito Hill. There would be no Union troops there. There would be no army to fight. There would only be desolation and the emptiness of deserted places, a blood-soaked region that held bad memories for Yankees and Confederates alike.

"Lou, remember when we had that truce with the North?" Brad asked.

"Yeah. I remember it didn't last long."

"About two months, I think."

"Then that damned Barrett let loose his pack of black dogs."

"Yep, good old Colonel Theodore H. Barrett of the 62nd Infantry."

"That was a Negro outfit," Gid said. "And we thought they were going to stay put in Brazos de Santiago."

"I got the full story from Ford when I last saw him," Brad said. "After he disbanded the cavalry under his command. Barrett had a full regiment and he was a glory hound, a politically appointed rascal who wanted to make a name for himself on the front lines."

"The Union had a lot of those boys," Randy said.

"Besides the Negroes in his regiment, Barrett had the 34th Indiana, the Morton Rifles, and some Texas cavalry commanded by Jack Haynes."

"He had a passel of artillery, too," Gid said.

"What you didn't know was that Barrett asked General E. B. Brown for permission to rattle some muskets on our flanks just so he could get some notoriety before the war ended. Well, his request was denied and he was told to just hold his position on his own hills."

"You mean he disobeyed orders?" Randy asked.

"Not only that," Brad said, "but Lieutenant Colonel Branson of the 34th Indiana raised Cain and begged Barrett not to countermand division orders."

"Barrett wanted himself some glory," Lou said. "That about right?"

"If you remember," Brad said, "Barrett ordered his Negro regiment to march on Palmito Hill at sunup. I'll never forget the date."

"Me neither," Gid said. "It was May 12th."

Lou and Randy both nodded. Hollie was hanging on every word.

"We were in Brownsville, I remember," Randy said. "Not that long ago."

"Yeah," said Brad. "Giddings opened up on the Negroes with rifle fire and held them back, then about dusk of that day, Giddings sent a rider to Brownsville. Colonel Ford sent out a bunch of couriers all over the place to every man jack in the outfit. He was madder'n hell that Barrett broke the truce. Rip had blood in his eye that night."

"But didn't General Slaughter want to turn tail and run?" Randy asked.

"Slaughter thought it was over," Brad said. "He figured Giddings would be overrun and Barrett would swarm all over Brownsville and chop us to pieces. He ordered a general retreat. Rip couldn't believe it until

Slaughter confiscated a civilian wagon and started loading it with his personal stuff."

"I saw him doing it that night, while you were inside with Rip Ford," Gid said. "I wondered what was going on."

"Rip was breathing fire by then," Brad said. "He told John Slaughter he'd already sent out couriers to beat the brush to round up all the scattered units of the cavalry and that he wasn't about to let Giddings down. Slaughter said, 'I'm ordering you and my army to retreat, Rip, and you are bound to obey that order.' "

"I'll bet Rip didn't like that much," Lou said.

"In fact," Brad said, "Rip told the general, 'You can go to hell if you wish. These are my men and I'm going to fight.' "

Gid, Randy, and Lou laughed, then Paco and Hollie joined in. "Rip said that?" Gid asked.

"He damned sure did," Brad said.

"And we saddled up at dawn," Gid said.

Lou shuddered visibly. "We rode straight for Palmito Hill."

"And we thumped the Yankees real good," Randy said. "Never lost a man."

"Barrett's artillery pieces went south, over the border," Brad said. "A lot of them, anyway, and my guess is that Thorne knows where those cannon are. I heard talk right after the battle."

"Do you think Thorne is going after those artillery pieces?" Lou asked.

"I sure as hell do," Brad said.

"And just what good will that do him?" Hollie asked.

Brad looked at her as if she had suddenly appeared out of nowhere. Then his face darkened and his eyes narrowed to slits.

"I think," he said, "that Thorne will blow everything in his path to kingdom come. I think he means to kill every Negro landowner from the Rio Grande to the Nueces."

"Can we stop him?" Hollie asked.

"We'll have to ride like hell," Brad said, "but we damned sure have to stop him or he's liable to start the war up all over again."

Five minutes later, Brad's small band was riding south to the Rio Grande. Their expressions were grim and the dust spooled up in their wake as they galloped toward a place that had already been drenched in blood, a place where the terrible war had ended; a place of death.

22

THE FOG HAD ROLLED IN FROM THE GULF OF MEXICO during the night, and it thickened just before dawn. Brad breathed a sigh of relief when Gid and Paco, sent ahead to scout Palmito Hill and the Rio Grande, rode up out of the curtain of brume to report.

"We got here in time, Major," Gid said. "We couldn't see nothing, but we could hear men talking, horses splashing across the ford dragging two cannon."

"How do you know they have cannon?" Brad asked.

"They was cussin' them field pieces, Brad. Paco, he got off his horse and walked up on 'em. He saw two cannon."

"That right, Paco?"

"I hear a man say two cannon were enough. One, he say, too much trouble to get more."

"Two probably are enough, with the number of men Thorne has," Brad said. "We don't have much time."

Gid cleared his throat. "Major, we don't have no time at all."

"What do you mean?"

"I heard someone ride up after they got the cannon across the river and report to Thorne hisself."

"Thorne had scouts out," Brad said. It was not a question.

"Yeah, I reckon. This scout hollered his report across the river to Thorne, so's I could hear him real good. He said we were six riders, one a woman, and called you by name."

"Did you recognize his voice?" Brad asked.

"I'd recognize that voice anywhere," Gid said. "It was Pete Jenkins, sure as shootin'."

"Pete was one of those who deserted and joined up with Vidal," Brad said.

"That's him. Damned traitor."

"He gave us fits, because he knew so much about the Cavalry of the West."

"I remember," Gid said.

"So he's with Thorne. Probably been with him all along."

"I reckon."

"Well, we're badly outnumbered," Brad said. "But we've got to stop Thorne from using those cannon."

"We were outnumbered that morning when we rode against Barrett's regiment," Lou said.

"Damned right," Randy agreed. "Beggin' your pardon, ma'am," he said to Hollie.

Brad remembered that day well. Rip Ford had been inspired; he had been superb. Barrett must have thought he had run right into a hornets' nest when the cavalry swooped down on him out of the fog of gunsmoke that hung in the air and decimated his ranks.

They rode to the sound of Giddings's guns, southwest to Palmito Hill on the Palo Alto plain. It took three hours after they left Brownsville to come upon the fighting. Palmito Hill was ringed with white smoke that clung to the ground because of the heavy damp air.

Giddings was pouring lead into Barrett's advancing skirmish line. Ford's scouts reported that the Indiana and Morton Rifles regiments had been sent into the inland brush by Barrett during the night. The men of these regiments were dog tired and Ford knew it. The humidity and the heat sapped the strength of many a foot soldier.

Ford led his cavalry into a cluster of thick brush that arced the edge of the plain. He dispatched infantry to harass the Union troops on the other flank, while his borrowed French artillery opened up on Palmito Hill.

Ford's skittery horse pranced around as the colonel shouted: "Men, we have whipped the enemy in all previous fights. We can do it again."

The troops, heartened by this display of heart and determination, loosed a rousing cheer that promptly drew Union fire down on the men in the thicket. Ford yelled "Charge," then led three hundred men straight into the Yankee flank. All the men in the cavalry yelled at the tops of their lungs. It was a chilling and a thrilling sound that could be heard for miles.

Screaming and shrieking like Apache warriors, the horsemen smashed into Barrett's skirmish line and broke it up. Yankees fled right and left, running for their lives. Brad and the others fired until their gun barrels were smoking hot, dropping the enemy until the ground was strewn with dead and wounded bluecoats.

The Indiana troops and the Morton Rifles from New York were terrified and confused. Barrett ordered a general retreat, but it was too late. And in his own confused state, he apparently forgot to call in his picket line.

Brad and the other cavalry troopers rode full bore into the Yankee lines and shot them to pieces. No less than three times during the seven-mile retreat toward Brazos de Santiago, Barrett tried to stop and fight, but Ford pressed him with his cavalry and brought along his horse artillery, which lobbed shells into the frightened and demoralized Yankees.

Every time Barrett halted and tried to fight back, Ford and the cavalry rode around them and chopped them up while the horse artillery fired shells with maddening accuracy into the Union ranks.

At dusk, Barrett's rear guard was staggering with ex-

*haustion and firing wildly with no certain targets in
sight. The cavalry kept circling and shooting holes in
the retreating army's ranks as they reached the salt waters of Boca Chica.*

*The Yankees waded across, splashing water like crip-
pled ducks. The color sergeant of the 34th Indiana
wrapped the regimental flag around his body and tried
to swim to Brazos Island. Randy leveled his rifle at the
man and shot him dead. Then Lou, Gid, and two other
men rode out and picked up the sodden flag. The entire
Confederate force cheered and Ford knew he had won
the battle and defeated Barrett's regiment without a single man killed.*

*To everyone's surprise, Slaughter, who had stayed be-
hind in Brownsville, rode up and ordered Ford to continue to punish the enemy.*

*"The battle's over with, General. I'm not going to
send my men to attack that island in the dark. They'll
all give up and surrender at first light."*

*"Damn you, Rip," Slaughter said, and then rode out
to within three hundred miles of the island. Cursing and
yelling, he drew his pistol and fired at the Yankees until
his gun was empty.*

"He's plumb crazy," Lou said.

"Poor bastard," Randy added.

Ford shook his head and walked away in disbelief.

"What a hell of an end to a great battle," Brad said.

"What a waste of ammunition," Ford said.

Brad made his decision. He knew what to do, but he
didn't know if it would work.

"Gather 'round and listen real careful," he said.

Paco, Hollie, Randy, and Lou crowded close to Brad
and Gid.

"Hollie, can you shoot from a horse?" Brad asked.

"Some."

"When the horse is running?"

"I don't know," she said. "Any advice?"

"Aim low, and don't shoot your horse," Brad said.

"Are we going to charge that bunch?" Gid asked.

"I'm going to charge," Brad said. "Just to pick off one or two. You'll all wait for me to get back. Stay about ten yards apart. When they start to shoot back, we're all going to ride back and forth, in and out, in two sections, shooting in to them."

"In this fog, we can't see much," Lou said.

"Which might just give us an edge," Brad said. "What we'll do is ride in straight lines, so we don't shoot each other. Back and forth, until I give the word to fall back. You'll fire at the sound of their weapons. If you hear a cannon go off, pour lead right straight at the sound."

"Might work," Randy said.

"Keep your cartridges handy. Load fast, shoot fast."

"We'll do 'er," Lou said.

"I am ready," Paco said.

"We're all ready," Lou said. "This waitin's gettin' to me."

"Load your rifles up, check your ammunition, and wait for me to get back," Brad said.

He jacked a shell into the chamber of his rifle and checked his pistols. Then he turned his horse and rode slowly toward Palmito Hill. The others murmured "good luck" to him and then were silent.

The fog parted, then closed back in again, swirling up and around Brad like some deadly shade. He rode slowly, quietly, using stealth and the fog to conceal his movement.

Soon he heard voices, fragments of disembodied phrases that he could not decipher. As he rode closer, he found he could make out the words, distinguish between different individuals. He heard the renegades talking about the two cannon and someone he took to be Thorne giving orders. He heard the creak of leather, the snap of reins, the ring of buckles, and the curses of men straining to find objects and tools in the dark.

Brad rode in very close, then reined up his horse. He sat there, listening for some time, isolating the voices,

determining where the men stood closer together. He
tried to peer through the fog, but it was too thick. He
knew he dared not get any closer, and he had to make
sure that, after he opened fire, he could move from his
flashes and get away in a hurry.

He drew in a deep breath and brought his rifle to his
shoulder. Then, focusing on the heaviest concentration
of voices, Brad squeezed the trigger. The rifle cracked
and bucked against his shoulder. A streak of bright orange flame spewed from the muzzle and he heard the
bullet sizzle through the air.

A man screamed in agony and Brad fired another shot
before squeezing his knees against his horse. The horse
sidled away to another position. Brad kept firing until
his rifle was empty, then sheathed it in its scabbard. He
turned his horse as rifle fire and shouting erupted several
yards away. Bullets whistled past him as he rode off,
back to where his companions waited.

Brad rode a zigzag course, the fog parting before him
briefly. When he saw the others, he reined to a stop,
pulled his rifle out of its scabbard, and began to reload.

"Hit anyone?" Gid asked.

"Hard to tell," Brad replied. "Randy, get started.
Move in close and watch yourself."

Randy, Gid, and Lou rode off into the fog.

"Paco, Hollie, follow me," Brad said, and rode off in
the opposite direction. The firing from Thorne's men
continued sporadically and Brad homed in on the sound
of gunfire. He turned toward it and began shooting, aim-
ing low, firing from the hip.

He saw flashes of orange flame, heard the shouts of
angry men. Seconds later, he heard Randy and the others
open fire and he saw the streaks of flame spewing from
their rifles, as well.

White smoke mingled with the fog as the shooting
continued on both sides. Brad and his pair passed
Randy's trio twice more before Brad called for them to

pull back. He was relieved to see that none of them had been hit.

"Fog's clearing some," he said. "We'll wait until we can see."

"I think we hit some of them," Gid said.

"I know I did," Lou said, "and I think Randy might have nailed a couple."

"I won't speculate about our bunch," Brad said, "but at least we put Thorne on the defensive."

"We gave him what for," Randy said.

"Let's move back to the brush for cover," Brad said.

No sooner had they all started to follow him, when they heard a hissing sound, followed by an explosion. They heard the whoosh of a cannonball slicing the air.

Hollie and Gid were still reloading their rifles when the ball hit the ground and exploded, filling the air with fire and shrapnel.

"Come on," Brad yelled, and spurred his horse.

As they reached the brush, the second cannon went into action and sent a ball whistling through the fog. It exploded several yards to their rear and left a thin path through the scrim of fog.

The sun began to spread light through the mist and fog as Brad and his companions melted into the brush.

That's when several bluecoats rose up on foot, their rifles all aimed at Brad and his followers.

Lieutenant Coy stepped up and said: "You're under arrest, Colonel Chambers. If you resist, my men are instructed to shoot to kill. Now, light down and surrender, sir."

Brad looked at the black hole of Coy's pistol and wondered what he had gotten himself into, and how in hell he was going to get himself out of it.

23

BRAD STEPPED DOWN FROM THE SADDLE SLOWLY AND faced his captor.

"Who in hell are you?" he asked.

Coy identified himself. Brad scanned the faces of the other soldiers and recognized some of them as those who had resupplied him at Little Thicket.

"You're making a big mistake, Coy. I'm under orders from General Sheridan."

"You mean you're in the Union Army?" Gid said. He shook his head.

"Just for this mission," Brad replied. "I didn't think you'd come with me if you knew."

"Well, I'm under orders from General Granger," Coy said with authority. "You, sir, are charged with killing a civilian at Hogg's Wells."

"Grimley? We didn't kill him. He was already dead when we got to Hogg's Wells."

"So you say."

The others all affirmed Brad's statement, including Hollie.

"You can't win this one," Brad said. "Now, I suggest you and your men come under my command. Abel

Thorne's on Palmito Hill and he's unlimbered two cannon against us."

"We heard cannon," Coy admitted. "Are you sure it's Thorne?"

"Positive. We tracked him here from Hogg's Wells. He's all stirred up now. Probably has eight or ten men in fighting shape. Your outfit could even the odds."

"I don't believe you entirely, Colonel, but maybe I believe this young woman some." He turned to Hollie. "Who are you, miss, and what are you doing on a military expedition?"

Hollie told him quickly about the Coopers, and her pa and brother. There was bitterness and conviction in her steady words. "Colonel Chambers has shown me the only kindness from soldiers since the Civil War began," she said.

"Well, Lieutenant," Brad said, "are you going to make a name for yourself by arresting me, or are you going to fight with some brave men and this woman to help me kill or capture Abel Thorne?"

Coy looked at Paco, who looked at Hollie, then nodded. Hollie smiled at him.

"I'm a civilian as well," Paco said, "and what Brad and Hollie say is true. The fat man was already dead when we see him. We did not kill him."

"All right, sir. You make a pretty convincing argument. If that's Thorne on Palmito Hill, then both General Sheridan and General Granger want him out of action. He's already done enough damage."

As if to punctuate the urgency of the situation, the two cannon roared in succession and the whistling balls landed less than two hundred yards from the brush.

"He's getting our range," Brad said. "You troops load up your rifles and get mounted. We'll have to attack once this fog lifts."

"Yes, sir," Coy said, and his men began to obey Brad's order. Brad climbed back into his saddle. He rode up to Hollie. "Thanks," he said. "You don't have to mix in this, you know. You can ride deeper into the brush and stay there until it's all over."

"I'm going to fight with you," she said.

"I hope you mean that the way I think you do."

"I do, Colonel."

"Don't start that. You can call me Brad."

"Only if you call me Hollie and not 'ma'am.' "

"All right, Hollie. Just follow my orders and don't get shot."

Coy rode up. "What's your plan, Colonel?"

"Those cannon are pointed straight at us. We'll split up into two groups. You and three of your men and two of mine attack on Thorne's right flank. I'll take the rest of your men and mine and cover the left flank."

"Sounds like a good plan."

"Don't think this is going to be easy, Coy. Thorne's men are all ex-soldiers, deserters, probably. They're well-armed and they are probably excellent shots."

"I'll take that into consideration," Coy said.

"Spread out," Brad commanded, "and take your positions. Don't charge the enemy until I give the command."

Brad gave one more order before he left to attack Thorne's left flank. "First, kill all their horses," he said. "I want Thorne cut off from all escape."

Coy saluted and the two groups split up as the sun rose in the eastern sky, burning off the fog.

Brad led his group from the brush and angled left, counting on the lingering fog to conceal his movements. Soon, he heard the rattle and clank of the cannon as men moved them from their former positions. He heard voices speaking just above a whisper, but couldn't make out any of the words.

The ten-pound Spencer repeating rifle in his hands felt light, even with its full capacity of seven rounds loaded into its spring-fed tubular magazine. The rifle was 47 inches long, but it could reach out to two thousand yards and was deadly accurate in its battle range of three hundred to five hundred yards.

As he drew closer to the voices, Brad lifted his right hand and motioned for his followers to fan out behind him. Then when he saw shadows through the fog, he pointed and looked around him to see if all his troops were in position. When they formed a file on his left, Brad stepped his mount forward, looped the reins around his saddlehorn, and brought the Spencer to his shoulder. He levered a cartridge into the chamber and drew a bead on one of the men standing beside the nearest cannon.

Brad squeezed the trigger and the rifle barked, breaking the eerie silence of morning. Then he heard the comforting crackle of rifles all along his flank as the others in his company opened fire a split second later.

The air filled with blossoms of white smoke, and he swung his rifle on the horses gathered behind the two cannon and started firing off rounds into their midst even as Thorne's men scrambled to mount up.

In the distance, he heard Coy's men engage Thorne on the opposite flank and the thrill of battle surged in his veins as he reloaded, a cumbersome task without the quick-loading box with its ten tubes.

Men in Thorne's cadre screamed, but soon some of them began to return fire. Brad heard Thorne, or someone, barking commands, and when he was reloaded, he shot a man trying to move one of the cannon around to bring it to bear on his position. He guided his horse with his knees as he rode in and out of the fog, picking off targets of horses and men. The smoke, mingled with the fog, began to form a thick ring around Palmito Hill much as it had been on that last battle of the war.

He dodged in and out of the gauze of fog, and as horses galloped past him, riderless, he knew that he and his men were winning. Rifles cracked all around him and he rode up on a man from Thorne's bunch swinging his rifle on Hollie as she rode into the thick of battle. Brad dropped the man and saw him throw his rifle into the air and collapse with blood streaming from a hole in his chest.

Close range now, and Brad sheathed the Spencer after reloading it and charged back in, a brace of pistols filling both his hands.

The fog continued to lift as Brad rode back in, close to the silent cannon. He saw the others in his flanking party close by, each following his lead, putting their rifles in their scabbards and drawing their pistols.

Brad shouted to them as they rode in: "If any of those men talk too fast or move too slow, shoot that man down."

The others gave a cheer and, as they rode in, Thorne's men began to scatter like quail flushed from a thicket. He shot the nearest man with the pistol in his left hand, then swung on another, who threw up both hands and dropped to his knees in surrender.

"Abe, they're on us," one man cried out.

"Abe, here they come," cried another, who started running toward the river after he threw down his rifle.

Hollie rode up close to Brad. "Did he say 'Abe'?" she asked.

"Probably what they call Abel Thorne."

"That's what I thought," she said.

Then Hollie spurred her horse and darted ahead of him before he could hold her back. He charged after her. Suddenly, she reined her horse to a halt and faced down four men hiding behind one of the cannon.

"You there," she called, "which one of you is Abe?"

None of the men moved or replied as Brad rode up to stop alongside her. He was joined in seconds by Paco and Gid. Then Coy and his men emerged out of the wisps of lingering fog and encircled the last of Thorne's men. Randy and Lou stared at the wounded and those standing with their hands raised in the air.

"Is this all of them?" Randy asked.

"I don't know," Brad said, "but one of these jaspers

is surely Abel Thorne, but with the beards I don't recognize any of them."

"I do," Hollie said, and stunned everyone there to silence.

"What?" Brad asked.

"I know them by their eyes and by their stink," she said.

"I don't understand," Brad said. "I didn't think you saw the men who killed your father and your brother."

"I didn't. But I've seen those three men before." She pointed them out with the barrel of her pistol. "During the war, these three were wearing Yankee uniforms when they came to our farm. Pa and Cal were gone. And these men raped me, one by one."

"You little bitch," Thorne said, and reached behind him. He pulled a hideout pistol and aimed it at Hollie as he lunged for her.

Brad didn't hesitate. He brought up the pistol in his right hand and cocked it on the rise. He fired, just as Thorne was squeezing the trigger of his small six-gun. Brad's shot caught him in the side and he twisted into a corkscrew fall. His pistol went off, sending a round into the ground. He looked up at Hollie and raised his pistol for another shot.

That's when she took deliberate aim with her own pistol and fired at point-blank range. The ball from her pistol tore through Thorne's mouth and jaw, leaving his face dripping with what looked like bloody rags.

Two of the men who had been standing with Thorne, Herbert Luskin and Orville Trask, started to run. Gid and Paco cut them down. The fourth man rushed to Thorne and knelt down beside him.

"I recognize that one," Coy said. "He's Benjamin Thorne, a slave smuggler. I saw his picture on a wanted poster once."

"Abe, Abe," Ben Thorne crooned, holding his son's bloody head in his hands. Thorne tried to speak, but his mouth was no longer intact, and his face contorted in pain.

"Look for stragglers," Coy ordered, and his men moved out, away from the group looking down on Ben Thorne and his dying son. Brad rode over to Hollie and leaned over. He put his arm around her waist. "I didn't know," he said.

"I never told anyone," she said. "Not even Pa or Cal."

"You've been carrying a hell of a lot on your shoulders, young lady."

Hollie turned and looked into his eyes. "I told you not to call me that anymore," she said.

"Sorry."

Then she reached over and touched him on the arm. "I know you didn't mean it in a bad way that time," she said. "In fact, I know you meant it in a nice way."

"I did, Hollie. Come on, let's get away from here. I need a smoke and you need to . . ."

"Cry?"

"Maybe."

"I think I've already cried it out. Those men got what they deserved. I won't cry for them."

"No. Neither will I. Come," he said.

They rode away from the smoke and the smell of death and over the small dunes toward the thicket. Hollie holstered her pistol and smiled at Brad.

"I liked it when you put your arm around me," she said. "I never thought I'd let a man do that to me again. Ever."

"Not all men are alike."

"I know that now. Riding with you, and your friends, I realized that there are decent men, good men. You're one of them, Brad."

"That's a mighty nice compliment, ma' . . . I mean, Hollie."

They both laughed, and then they dismounted and sat on the ground. They were still talking when Gid rode up on them.

"We found some whiskey, Brad. Everybody wants to celebrate. We whupped 'em good, just like before."

"I know," Brad said.

"Well, you comin' or not?"

Brad opened his mouth to reply, but just then Hollie touched him on his arm. It was a soft touch, light as a feather, but it was as strong as if she had clamped him in a vise.

"We'll be along directly, Gid. You go on."

"Well, there's plenty of whiskey, but don't you be too long. I've got me a powerful thirst."

Brad looked at Hollie, looked deep into her eyes, and felt himself falling into their cool, serene depths.

"So do I, Gid," he said. "So do I."

Gid cleared his throat in embarrassment. He turned his horse and rode away. He knew damned well that Brad wasn't talking to him when he said that. Knew it all along, he did, and couldn't nobody tell him no different.

He licked his lips. As for himself, he did have a powerful thirst.

But then, war, a battle, a good scrap, did that to a man, Gid reasoned, and he put spurs to his horse and rode toward the place they called Palmito Hill, gone silent with the sunrise just as it had on that last day of the Civil War.